Prince Eli

By

C. M. Padilla

I dedicate this book to my children, my wife, my mother, and especially my son Eli. He has been my hope and the main reason for keeping my life together. I thank him because, though he cannot yet know it, without him my life would be in pieces.

Acknowledgements

I humbly thank God for giving me the opportunity to write this book.

My beloved wife is my main inspiration and main encouragement. Without her, this book would not be a book, and I am so thankful to her.

We are both deeply grateful to our editor Julie Nierenberg for her passion and dedication in the process of preparing our manuscript, for believing in us and encouraging us to go ahead and step forward with the story of Prince Eli.

Some of the events written in this book are inspired by biblical stories.

"Let me tell you one last thing," continued Master Joed. "Don't put limits on your dreams. Use everything you've been given as you search and accomplish the purpose of your life. In this way you will affect the Universe in your favor. The Universe is no more than an infinite warehouse where all the dreams of men sit on shelves. But very few valiant men claim what belongs to them. Be you one of those valiant men! Fight with courage and with vigor until you get there and don't hesitate when circumstances seem adverse."

C. M. Padilla

Chapter I

In the Age of Kings and Queens there were Seven Kingdoms that stood as one Empire ruled by the great King Alexis.

Much like Solomon in his time, he was blessed with wisdom, wealth, and power to rule. King Alexis had been adorned by the very heavens above, kissed with the blessing of the Creator and guarded by the Divine Army of Heaven.

His favor rested only on his obedience to these celestial creatures, but—being like any other man—there came a day when Alexis' disobedience cost him everything. It rang through the celestial skies and clamored in the ears of the Creator Jhaveh, and the rule of King Alexis was no more.

The king's heart beat stubbornly against the visions and desires of Jhaveh. He behaved instead according to his own ideas of what he believed his Creator wanted and needed. In fact, in his mind he no longer needed the Creator to inspire him or guide him.

So it was that in the last years of King Alexis' reign a man sent by Jhaveh to deliver a holy decree found himself at the threshold of the ruler's royal throne room. He swung open both of the heavy doors, his plain gray robe dragging on the ground behind him.

The King and all his men—the generals and members of the royal court—stood gathered around the throne in a heated discussion, but all at once they turned their heads to the sound of the door handles forcefully slamming against the walls.

The hooded man pressed through the threatening and offensive stares of the other men and advanced toward the throne, his eyes unwavering as they stared into King Alexis' eyes. The man's shoes clacked in rhythm with his staff on the marble floor, echoing defiantly against the stillness, until he finally stopped at the center of the room.

"Who are you?" asked the king, raising the tone of his voice with contempt. "You dare interrupt a royal council meeting? Show yourself!"

Geordano, first general to the king gripped his sword, ready to make the man regret his mistake, but King Alexis motioned for General Geordano to stop.

The man lifted his hands to his face and slowly pulled back his hood, revealing his identity.

Upon seeing the man's countenance all in the room went straight to their knees without hesitation and bowed their heads in reverence.

"Bartknap!" the king gasped, slowly rising from his throne. "Bless this servant of Jhaveh!" he said, lowering himself to his left knee in front of the man. "What matter brings you to my house, Prophet of the Lord?"

Tall and gangly, Bartknap was no match in a fight, but in matters of the Spirit his presence alone commanded respect. He was loyal only to Jhaveh. The prophet rested his hand on King Alexis' shoulder, looking him squarely in the eyes, "Great King! I have not come to your house today to bless you." Slowly he continued walking.

King Alexis stood and pivoted toward the prophet, "What has brought you to my house then?"

"I was sent to ask you but one question."

"Okay... I'm listening."

The prophet began first with a story:

"In a faraway land there was a very rich man with two sons. One morning, the man ordered his two sons to work in one of the fields of his vineyard. The first son told his father that he would go work in the vineyard, but then did not go. The second son, when asked, did not want to go, but later, after his father left, decided to obey and went to the vineyard to work."

"Now, here is the question: Which of the two sons carried out the will of his father and obeyed?"

"The second son—of course," the king answered quickly.

"Wisely have you answered, King Alexis," the prophet said. "Three days ago I came to your house with specific orders from Jhaveh. I prophesied to you concerning the desire of Jhaveh to expand your kingdom and the True Worship to the end of the lands inhabited by men. But you have resolved in your heart not to do the will of the one who created you!"

The king sat down slowly on his throne, leaned forward, stroked his beard, held his hand there for a moment, and then finally hung his head, resting it on his fingertips, and let out a deep breath.

"You are that first son, King Alexis. You have disobeyed the will of your Lord," the prophet said.

The prophet began again, "Listen now, to the words of Jhaveh:

'I anointed you king of all men. I saved you from the hands of your enemies. I gave you glory and power, and if this were not enough, I would have added to you more. Why then did you count as nothing the word of your Lord, disobeying what you were commanded to do? Now, because you have trespassed against me, the sword will never leave your house. Truly I tell you, the evil and punishment you have welcomed in your house, I will display in broad daylight, in front of all your people. All this will come to pass because you have secretly decided in your heart to ignore the words of your Lord."

The king sat, stunned, eyes wide and bewildered, but then, casting his sight downward, a look of recognition came over him. "I have transgressed against Jhaveh."

The prophet continued, "Jhaveh has also seen the repentance that now rests in your heart and because of this, I tell you, from your own house a redeemer will arise. The redeemer will wipe away the disobedience that covers your house in disgrace. His heart will be pure, and he will lead this empire with great power to victory."

Having no other words to say, the prophet left.

Chapter II

In three years' time, just as spoken by the prophet, the awaited birth of redemption took place.

It was in the eleventh hour of the night. The sky was cloaked in a peculiar and eerie fog. Even stranger was the heavy and suffocating darkness that seemed to press down on the city of La Ataviada, closing in on its residents.

Nonetheless, the full moon hung serene in her expanse of the heavens, immobile, holding her breath, anticipating the arrival of a new life. She cast her light through the window of Queen Megdany as if to peek in on this most special delivery.

"Be strong, My Lady!" Sarai, the midwife exclaimed, hyperventilating along with the queen. "You're almost there!" Two helpers were fanning the queen to cool her as she labored.

Beads of sweat poured down Queen Megdany's face, and her fingers locked in a vice-like grip around the nurse's hand. She pursed her lips again, ready to push, exhaled deeply, and then quickly inhaled again. An intensely agonizing pain shot through her body, "Aahhhh!"

Needing comfort, the queen asked with great difficulty between breaths, "Where is the king?"

"Your husband is outside the room, My Lady," responded Sarai, "but don't think about that right now. Just keep pushing. Your baby is about to be born."

With each moan and scream of pain the king dug his heels harder into the floor and quickened his nervous pacing outside her chamber door.

Suddenly, General Geordano walked up to the king with heavy strides. "My Lord, the other generals and I sense that this evening something dreadful is hanging in the atmosphere, as if some supernatural thing is taking place outside the palace."

"What do you think it is?" asked the king.

"I'm not sure, Your Majesty," answered General Geordano, "but the other generals and I have had several reports from the townspeople that the whole city feels as if it's walled in by some kind of evil, and the animals in their stables are very unsettled. Everyone is on edge."

After taking a minute to think, the king answered, "General Geordano, I trust you with my life, and if I could I'd go with you. But at this moment I must be with my wife. I have faith in you to handle everything as I would. You and the other generals must take control of this situation."

General Geordano answered, "Yes, My Lord," and then swiftly went on his way.

Geordano made haste and gathered the other generals, "Queen Megdany is about to give birth and the king is with her. We must secure our townspeople and everything inside these walls. I believe it necessary to send men outside the city to surround the walls and set a 200-meter perimeter."

Inside the palace, the queen's chamber door opened. Sarai appeared, wiping her bloody hands on her dress skirts. Seeing the blood, King Alexis' face froze. He could only lift his eyebrows to ask if everything was alright. The midwife drew a slow smile and nodded her head to assure him everything went just fine.

The king sighed and raised his arms to Heaven, praying with relief and gratitude.

"Thank you, My Creator, for the new life you have given into my hands today." Tears of joy streamed from the corners of his eyes. Softly he walked into the room where his queen was lying in bed. Watching her with adoration, he saw that although she was weak and tired she held the newborn prince in her arms.

King Alexis sat down next to his wife on the bed and gave her a hug and kiss on the cheek. He lifted the baby from her arms, raised his son to Heaven, and exclaimed: "You will be named Eli!"

The little prince let out his first cry.

Not a moment later, a gust of cold wind burst through their room, blowing out the flames of every candle except for the one lighting the queen's bedside. A dreadful shriek filled the air, echoing down every street and into every home, like a demon in anguish.

Never again was there a night surrounded with such mystery and such destiny as there was on the arrival of Prince Eli.

Chapter III

While the birth of the young prince brought much joy, Bartknap's prophecy was only partially fulfilled, and so the prince's birth also brought a disturbing sadness. The great King Alexis, Ruler of the Seven Kingdoms must fall.

Prince Eli was just nine years old when life all around him began to crumble and crack. Sometimes he would eavesdrop on his father, ear pressed to the wall or eyes peeking between closed doors. Eli could feel the worry and trepidation his father dared not reveal to his son.

While gallivanting through the streets of La Ataviada, whispers and rumors found their way to his tiny, innocent ears. Again, he could sense that some foreboding event was coming.

Prince Eli was not afraid, and he did not bother his parents with these inklings or dismiss them for being trivial in a child's world. Instead, he was perfectly and strangely calm.

And finally the beginning of the end came to pass.

"We have to do something, My Lord!" General Geordano pleaded fervently with his king, hammering his fist on the table. "If we don't fight back, the allied forces of King Jonaed will reach La Ataviada and then all of our Empire will fall to his power!" Geordano felt perplexed by the king's indifference.

Geordano continued, "A platoon of our soldiers was able to escape from the South and reported Jonaed's troops were far too many, and also that Faust and Sonaguera have already been completely overtaken... What is your answer, My Lord?"

General Geordano was a tall, strong soldier. His wavy, sandy brown hair and soft honey brown eyes offset his square jaw and thick, brooding, prominent eyebrows, giving the impression that he was both noble and wild.

Undoubtedly, his allegiance was to the king, and he carried many burdens concerning the kingdom. He was faithful and loyal and, most of all, no matter how hopeless things looked, he never gave up. This was precisely why Jhaveh had chosen him to serve as general to King Alexis. General Geordano could see the good in all things, even if the good could not yet be seen by others.

Second General Melany, confirming the need for an answer added, "Emissaries sent by our officers in Creta reported that Saba has also been invaded, and all our troops situated in Creta will surrender, because King Jonaed's army strengthens in numbers by the day, Your Majesty."

General Levy paced around the council room, exasperated. He tried not to think of what might happen if Jonaed somehow defeated their armies. Swooping in between the others gathered around the king, he demanded "General Geordano is right, My Lord! We have to act as soon as possible!"

King Alexis pushed the voices of the generals away, after listening carefully to all they said. Under normal circumstances they would not have to reason with him.

The king knew the fulfillment of the prophecy had come. He tried to hide his sadness, knowing that the decision to attack was not his to make. Neither winning nor losing was in his control. His generals begged and pleaded for an answer, but he could not give what they requested.

Finally, taking a deep breath, King Alexis, for the first time since the meeting began, looked into the desperate, impatient faces of his valiant generals, and spoke.

"This morning, my dear generals, the Council of Twelve Elders gathered to consult our Lord Jhaveh about this matter. You know that the power of our Empire comes from Him. Therefore, we must wait for the answer before acting. He is the one that has given us so many years of peace, and He is also the one that now brings us war. So whatever His desire may be, that is what we shall do."

After a small pause the King continued,

"Now, go back to your respective posts until I receive the instructions. I will send messengers to each of you letting you know when and where we will meet. Don't spend any time being anxious about this matter. Instead, be patient and wait."

In the royal dormitory of Prince Eli, a sobbing Queen Megdany softly caressed the face of her sleeping son.

She had premonitions of the terrible things that were about to happen and wanted to be with the prince as much as possible.

"What destiny awaits you, son of mine?" she asked between quiet sobs. She leaned over the bed that cradled him, watching him sleep.

"I wish I could freeze this moment in time," she said to herself.

Three years before, Jhaveh came to her while she slept. He reminded her of the prophecy Bartknap had given the king: "The king and his kingdom must fall."

Tears rolled down her cheeks as she recalled the judgment that had been handed down, but for a flash she held her breath, hearing the one single word Jhaveh had spoken with such certainty that now in her weakness she was renewed with hope and the dimly burning flame of her faith was reignited.

"Redeemer," He had said.

Jhaveh continued, "Mickail, one of the Divine Army's commanders, will come to rescue your son from the war and safely take him out of the Empire for the time of two perfect ages."

The revelation settled in her a feeling of security for the future of the Empire. Yet, in the back of her mind she worried about her son, knowing how young, innocent, and still helpless he was, but she shoved the idea out of her head declaring, "Jhaveh will protect you, my son." She forced a deep, slow smile.

Engrossed in her thoughts, she didn't notice King Alexis had entered the room until she heard him whisper in her ear, "I love you, queen of mine. I don't know what would become of me if I didn't have you."

"I love you too, My Lord," she said turning to face him. She gently stroked his face, searching his eyes for the answers to all of her questions.

"Let me shelter myself in you," said King Alexis. "Your heart has always been my palace of safety."

At his words, she sank herself lovingly onto his chest. "This is the end of our kingdom, My Lord," she said softly. "Our Empire will fall."

"I know," King Alexis responded. "I knew someday that I would have to face the consequences for deliberately disobeying the desire of Jhaveh."

"Being a man, I believed so stubbornly that the True Worship had traveled to its end and could go no further. I was ignorant. I paid no attention to Jhaveh's desire. He asked me to reveal the Mystery to all men on Earth, and I decided in my heart to do nothing. I have waited for these consequences with sadness for many years," he added.

"Our son will survive," she said, still resting her head on his chest. "Jhaveh came to me in my dreams. He told me Mickail, one of the Divine Army's commanders, would come to our house at the right moment and take our son to the White Mountains of the South where the Yepoc Indians live. He will be protected from the evil of Blackfire. For two perfect ages he will be educated in wisdom and be prepared to rule the Empire."

A light knock on the door interrupted them.

"You may enter," said the king.

The palace herald came into the room, bowing reverently, and said, "The Council of the Eldest requests your presence with urgency, Your Majesty. You must attend to the Holy Place."

The King took the hand of his beloved wife and gave her a kiss on the cheek as a short goodbye.

"Order my transportation immediately, herald!" the king commanded as he left the room.

Traveling on horseback, King Alexis and his guards arrived at the Holy Place in the tenth hour of the night. The king dismounted and climbed the stairs. He entered through a long and narrow passage, its walls engraved with sacred scriptures.

Finally arriving in the main room, the scene before him was daunting. A semicircle of twelve elders awaited his arrival. Each the twelve was unblemished. Their skin shone with clarity, their long white tunics pristine, and even their expressions were perfect; they neither hid nor gave away anything. They simply sat stone silent in chairs made of silver and acacia wood and adorned with precious jewels.

The walls and ceiling were made of a thick semitransparent glass so that moonlight was the only thing that could see into this secret meeting. The floor too was made of glass, and was supported by many petrified trunks of acacia wood.

King Alexis was overwhelmed with a sense of trepidation. Walking to the center, he bowed with deep reverence and said:

"I am here. You requested my presence."

Bartknap, the eldest prophet, rose from his chair and said, "King Alexis, this is what Jhaveh has to tell you at this time:

'A crown of glory was given to you. Jhaveh entrusted to you the power and dominion over all creatures that exist, in order that his truth and desire would extend to the furthest corners and peoples of the earth.

Your spirit has been weighed and been found wanting, because, a seed of pride began to grow in your heart. Your pride produced disobedience. In your actions, Jhaveh found iniquity. You must be held accountable for what you have done. Therefore, your kingdom has been taken from your hands and a foreign king will sit on your throne. He will slaughter your people without mercy. Your life and the life of your queen will be demanded of you before the war is over.'"

The elder paused, and the king bowed his head, sadly acknowledging what he heard.

"You must leave—" continued the elder, "go from this place. You will not be able to come back. It will be hidden until the times of Redemption. Love your wife, your son, and your people, since the time you have left under this sun is short. On the third day from today, at sunrise, you will leave for war."

King Alexis left the council chambers and went away from the Holy Place.

While the king and his guards descended the Sacred Mountains on their mounts, a thick cloud appeared, sent from Heaven to hide the Holy Place from the eyes of men. A sword of fire appeared, flying wildly in all directions, to protect the entrance of the Holy Place from intruders.

The king watched the trail disappear behind them, as the men and horses wound down the mountainside. Flowers and grass sprouted and quickly grew to cover the path so that no man could find the way leading to the Holy Place.

King Alexis marveled at what he saw, but after a while a stinging pain replaced his amazement. The deep intimacy he shared with his Creator and with the Council—like the trail—disappeared. Emptiness and loneliness spread through his entire being. The king felt cold.

He raised his eyes to the full moon high in the sky, displaying her beauty and calm presence over the firmament. Two thick tears slid down his cheeks as he remembered all the years of peace and glory his kingdom had enjoyed, up until now. The sorrow he felt made him want to go back in time and obey the orders given to him by Jhaveh so many years ago.

If only I had obeyed back then, he said to himself. *None of this would be happening.*

Over and over, a question rolled around in his mind: *Why does forgiveness have to be so complicated?*

Truly, no man on Earth, no matter how powerful, can avoid the consequences of his actions. Sinking deeper into his thoughts, Alexis arrived at a conclusion: *The Universe subjects all men to the divine laws that Jhaveh put into existence at the beginning of all things. This subjection is unavoidable. No man can say, "Blessing or misery has come to my life without reason, and all men will reach the same forgiveness or the same punishment, according to their actions."*

Understanding the weight of this truth, he resolved, *I will fight until the last drop of my blood is spilled.* Entering the doors of the city, he continued, *My people deserve nothing less. My disobedience has caused all this to pass.*

Arriving at the palace, the king immediately called for his generals to discuss plans for war.

"I believe the desert of Pespire is the land where we will fight this war, My Lord," General Geordano said. "All of our troops in the South are completely under King Jonaed's control. By the time we get there, our army of the East will be defeated too."

"But if we hurry, we can still save our troops in the West and use them to fight on our side," added General Troy.

"How many men do we have available?" asked the king.

"We have 20,000 men in the Imperial Army, My Lord," responded General Geordano. "They can be ready to fight in two days. Rumors of war have spread rapidly, and villagers are arriving in the city by the hundreds to protect their families behind these walls."

"Most of the soldiers around the city are already preparing for war, My Lord," added General Levy.

"What plans do we have to protect the city?" asked the king.

"One of us will have to stay in La Ataviada to protect the queen and the prince, My Lord," answered General Melany immediately.

"Also, I believe it is wise for us to send a group of emissaries to the kingdoms of Parma and Ilanga immediately, My Lord," said General Troy. "Our officers in the West need to receive orders as soon as possible. Time is not our best friend at present."

"Of course," said General Geordano, affirming General Troy.

The king heard everything the generals had to say. He fixed his eyes on them and with profound respect said, "Brothers of mine, soldiers of the Empire, your hearts are those of noble warriors. It would truly be an honor for me to spill my blood fighting by your side in this battle. Let it be done the way you have planned. Let Jhaveh lead us to victory!"

"General Geordano!" the king continued, "Prepare the Imperial Army. We will leave for the desert of Pespire at sunrise on the third day from now.

"General Melany, to you I give the orders to protect La Ataviada. 3,000 men will stay under your command. Guard this house with your life. Take care of my queen and my son.

"General's Troy and Levy! Take a platoon of soldiers and go west to the kingdoms of Parma and Ilanga. Gather the troops and meet us in the oasis of Kaukira nine days from now.

"Now, my desire is that all of you, and every single soldier going to war, enjoy your families for the next two nights. Jhaveh be with us all."

Then he told them to leave. After bowing, each of the generals left to accomplish their orders.

Waiting until the room was empty, King Alexis lifted his sight again to the ceiling. He desired with all his strength that everything that was happening wasn't true.

He began to think again of all the blood that would be spilled because of his disobedience. Dropping to his knees, he asked forgiveness from his Creator once again, depositing into his prayers every single piece of his heart.

Peace would not be found in the king's heart from this day forward. He could not stop asking why his repentance and regret were not enough to stop these events.

Chapter IV

Typical joyful evenings in La Ataviada—the laughter of children running and playing in the streets, the buzz of parents sitting outside talking, elders in the plazas telling their nostalgic tales, and lovers walking the gardens professing their love to the four winds— were gone. Instead, fear had taken over, patrolling up and down the streets, closing in on the townspeople. The streets were lonely. Not even the sound of a cricket's melody could be heard.

A terrible feeling of dread filled the hearts of La Ataviada's people. Thick clouds hid the stars in the firmament, and the fragile light of the moon appeared only in their fleeting passage. The pressing darkness weighed heavily on everyone.

The Empire had successfully evaded war for so long, and the idea of it was unfathomable to its people. Families gathered to worship Jhaveh, asking for their lives and the lives of the men going off to war the next day.

The townspeople and the natural world united to spend the night mourning for the men who would fall in battle.

The soldiers cherished their wives, children, brothers, sisters, and parents whom they would leave behind the following day. Family traditions were celebrated in bittersweet silence and sorrow instead of with joy.

In her royal chamber, Queen Megdany prayed on her knees, supporting her elbows on the bench facing the window. She begged Jhaveh for mercy, saying, "Oh Lord, mercy... mercy."

She began to think of all the things she was going to miss. Her loving arms would no longer embrace her son. Her hands would not caress his cheeks, nor would she be able to secretly watch him playing so carefree under the roof of the palace.

What caused her the most pain was that she would not see him grow from a boy into a man. With that thought she burst into full sobbing and prayed again for the mercy of Jhaveh.

King Alexis stood in the doorway, silently observing his wife's desperation. His heart ached. His beloved wife and partner, a gift given to him from the heavens, would be taken from him without mercy. After tonight he would never again lay eyes on her. A profound sorrow and sadness sat in his heart like hard and heavy boulders. What was done was done, and nothing but Jhaveh could change the events already set into motion.

He kneeled next to her, placing his arm around her. "Jhaveh will protect him," he whispered in her ear. "He won't let anything bad happen to him. I love you." He stared into her eyes for a long moment and then finally helped her to her feet.

"I love you too, My Lord," she responded, still crying. "I love you always, and I will love you even after the day of my death."

He took her hands softly in his own and then embraced her. King Alexis cried with his queen. He pulled back from her, placed his hand underneath her chin, and looked into her eyes. "I want to give you something," he said and then gave her a kiss that he would never be able to give again, even if he lived. His kiss discharged all the power of love contained in his soul, emptying him completely and sealing her lips eternally, so that none of his love would escape. The kiss was the final pact, until death, just like they had promised in the Holy Place before Jhaveh. The king desired with all his might to have the power to open a path in time and space that would take him to eternity, along with his beloved wife, never again to be separated.

"This night is our last night together, my love," he said putting his hands around her waist. "Tomorrow evening I will join the generals and the army outside the city walls."

"What's going to happen to the people in the city?" she asked, wiping away her tears.

"General Melany is staying to protect La Ataviada," he answered. "3,000 men will stay in the city under her command. Tonight, love of mine, I only want to enjoy you and my son. Tomorrow I will leave, to be far away from your arms and your warmth. Tonight, let me love you without words."

The queen brushed her lips against her husband's and again they blended in a kiss of profound love, baptized by tears, knowing this would be the last night they would spend together.

Early the next morning, the loud hoof beats of the horses pounding the streets of the city left no doubt that war was imminent. People leaned out their windows to salute the marching squadrons. Children ran down the streets, looking up at the soldiers and dreaming that someday they could be just like them, valiant and strong, attired in shining warrior armor.

On the outskirts of the city, General Geordano and officers of the Empire organized the men and horses, the archers, and the foot soldiers by platoons. The last straggling families from surrounding villages made their way through the gates of La Ataviada. The soldiers saw their families to a safe place inside the city walls, quickly said goodbye, and headed back to report to General Geordano.

Inside the city walls, General Melany assembled the guard that would stay behind to protect La Ataviada. She gave special instructions to her men that Queen Megdany and Prince Eli be protected at all costs. She also commanded them to prepare the escape route and secret passage that led to a small fortress on the outskirts of the North Mountains.

Generals Troy and Levy went west. They would not arrive until sunset of the second day and they would have very little time to put together 12,000 men to form the army of the West. They would not stop on the way, not even to rest, because of their strict orders to be at the oasis of Kaukira by sunrise of the ninth day.

Inside the palace, King Alexis worshipped Jhaveh. He was lying face down on the floor in front of the altar he had built to honor the Creator. The king of the Empire was reduced to nothing—the most humble man on Earth, asking that the blood spilled in battle would be little. The king fervently prayed for his people, not even thinking of himself. He already knew his fortune and could do nothing to change it.

Night fell, and in their encampment outside the walls, the soldiers started fires to keep warm. Sitting in silence, each one thought of what was ahead. One soldier, breaking the stillness, began telling a story about a king who ruled the Empire long ago.

"The line of pharaohs enslaved our fathers for many years," the soldier said. "Then a king, chosen by Jhaveh, came to rescue them. Jhaveh ordered the king to call down plagues upon the people of the pharaohs, and when the pharaohs finally couldn't take anymore, the king reclaimed our people, liberating them from slavery. By the hand of Jhaveh, he led them to the sea and opened it up to its floor to let the people of Jhaveh across."

Another soldier took his turn and recalled a story his father had passed down to him. The light of the fire gleamed in his eyes as he said, "There was a king who killed a giant named Goliath, who was five meters tall. He used only three stones and sent the enemy running!"

"1,000 men were killed with only the jaw of a camel!" another soldier said.

The night continued in this way. Soldier after soldier told about the great kings of the past who were used by Jhaveh to save His people. They were humble men, honored and favored by Jhaveh because of their obedience.

Enchanted by the feats of past kings, their stories reached a mystical place that whispered into the ears of the celestial, and their tales turned to the Divine Army. Their stories had been passed down to them from their parents and told of great and powerful angels riding winged lions who lived in Heaven, warriors under the command of Jhaveh.

In the main tent, things were much different. General Geordano and the officers discussed strategies for war.

"Welcome, Your Majesty," everyone said, inclining themselves before King Alexis as he entered the royal tent.

The king walked to the center of the tent where the maps lay on a table lit by hanging lamps. General Geordano and the officers hurried to open a space around the table for the king.

"What news do you have, General?" the king asked.

"We received information on the state of the invasion, My Lord," responded General Geordano. "The enemy armies invaded the kingdom of Creta. We believe their plan is to regroup in the desert of Pespire and attack Parma and Ilanga, and, finally, La Ataviada. We also received information that their army exceeds 100,000 men, My Lord."

The king said, "With that number of soldiers it will take several days for them to get to the desert of Pespire. We will have fifteen days' advantage over them before they reach Kaukira. That's more than enough time to regroup our armies of the West. At least we have that time in our favor."

"If you allow me, Your Majesty," said one of the officers named Galel. He paused in silence, waiting for the king's approval to speak.

The king motioned with his hand for Galel to proceed.

"I think if we hurry we can ambush them in the Canyon of La Gioconda," continued officer Galel. "King Jonaed's troops are coming from the East. When they come through the canyon, if we have 2,000 men posted on the canyon walls, we can surprise them. Likewise with the troops that are coming from the South, in the jungle of Karatasca—if we send soldiers ahead of us to ambush them before they get to the desert of Pespire we will reduce their troops considerably. The numbers will be more evenly matched."

The king stood, thinking for a moment and analyzing the officer's suggestion.

"I think this is an excellent idea," affirmed General Geordano. "If we reduce their troops in these two key places, we could have a very good possibility of victory."

The king observed the maps and carefully listened to his officers.

"What report do we have from the West?" asked the king.

"Nothing more, My Lord," General Geordano answered. "Troy and Levy will not arrive at their destination until tomorrow evening. Once they arrive, they will only have three days to regroup the armies of the West."

"How many men exactly are we counting on in the West?" asked the king.

"Approximately 12,000 men between the troops of Parma and Ilanga, My Lord," General Geordano answered.

The king turned around and addressed General Geordano, "Very well, General. I think we have a plan."

He paused before concluding, "Sound the horn of the sentinel tomorrow at the fifth hour."

General Geordano and all the officers went to their tents to rest. Tomorrow they would begin a very long march.

In the early hours of the morning, the horn of the sentinel sounded.

"Forward!" yelled King Alexis. The army began the journey to Pespire.

Meanwhile in the East, on the other side of the Empire, King Jonaed crushed the armies of Creta. Officers were taken as prisoners, governors decapitated, and villages destroyed by fire. Blood was everywhere. Women and children were spared, but not a single able-bodied man remained at large.

"King Jonaed, My Lord, we have just received information from one of the enemy soldiers. We believe King Alexis' army may be planning an ambush at Giaconda and Karatasca," said Eduen, King Jonaed's personal advisor.

"Well done," Jonaed answered and smiled at Eduen with deep satisfaction. He informed his officers of the new plans and quickly moved onward to confront the Royal Army of King Alexis.

Eduen was an evil sorcerer. There was not a single vile act he was incapable of doing. His abysmal black eyes were recessed into his skull, and his skin was tinged with the most pallid color and felt cold to the touch. His face was always covered with a black hood, and he concealed himself from head to toe.

Although Eduen was Personal Counselor to King Jonaed, he pledged his true service to his god, the Blackfire.

This Blackfire was unlike any beast. He was the Lord of Darkness and Evil. And just as Eduen did, Blackfire desired total control and widespread destruction. He strategically placed Eduen at the side of King Jonaed to whisper in his ear a declaration of war against the people of Jhaveh—against the Empire of the Seven Kingdoms.

Chapter V

The sun appeared on the horizon of the ninth day, as King Alexis and his Royal Army arrived at the oasis of Kaukira.

"General Geordano, make sure all soldiers are refreshed with water," ordered the king.

Generals Troy and Levy, and the army of the West, joined the king's forces assembled at the oasis. The generals went straight to the officers' tent.

"Welcome, Generals. Well done," said the king. "You have acted as you were ordered."

"Your Majesty," the generals said as they kneeled in front of the king.

"Please stand up. Tomorrow before sunrise, General Troy, you will lead 1,500 men to Karatasca. General Levy, you will lead 1,500 men to La Gioconda. It is imperative you set up an ambush at these places before King Jonaed's army arrives. We will all leave together at sunrise tomorrow. You will ride ahead to make sure the ambush is successful. We will arrive on foot three days later."

"As you order, My Lord," responded the generals in unison while raising their right hands to their chests.

"Go and select the men you want to take with you and then rest for the evening. You have another long journey ahead of you," King Alexis concluded.

"Your Majesty," the generals said and then left.

During the three-day march through the desert, King Alexis awaited news of their planned ambush of King Jonaed's forces. And indeed, the news finally came as they met up with the Royal Army's earlier dispatched contingent, or what remained of it.

"Hail, My Lord!" It was General Levy who addressed his king.

"What news do you have, General?" asked King Alexis.

"We have failed, My Lord! They knew, Your Majesty. Somehow they knew about the ambush. We have lost more men," Levy said with thorough disappointment.

The king remained silent for a moment before he asked, "And what of the enemy now, General Levy?"

"Your Majesty, I am afraid they will pursue us here. I can't say how soon they'll arrive," General Levy answered. "What shall we do?"

"We will be soldiers. We will confront Jonaed's army and we will hold nothing back. We will make camp here and wait for them," King Alexis answered resolutely. He remembered the promise he made to his people and knew he would give them nothing less than every drop of blood he had. He resolved in his soul to be the king that Jhaveh had created him to be, till his last breath.

Addressing General Geordano the king said, "Order the army to halt and make camp, and be sure to set around it a perimeter of 1,000 meters. Also, I want a general report every two hours."

"As you order, My King," responded General Geordano.

King Alexis and his army remained encamped for two days. On the morning of the third day, one of the sentinels saw on the horizon a flash of light, like the rays of the sun reflecting off a mirror. He saw another flash and another, until the flashes visibly became a vast army; the enemy shields were ablaze with the sun's blinding reflection.

The sentinel took a deep breath and exhaled. "So here it is," he told himself. Without any hesitation, he mounted his horse and rode to the Royal Army's camp to convey the message. "Alert! Alert!" he yelled. "The enemy is here!"

The men, having seen the king's determination, carried in their hearts the same courage. They anticipated this moment. The king and the soldiers were prepared. No chaos, no disorder, just thousands of men united in one heart and one mind, ready to take down their enemy.

King Alexis rode his horse through the ranks of his men, raised his sword to Heaven and yelled, "Soldiers of the Empire! The day to fight for the integrity of our people and our kingdom has arrived. Lift your heads high. Fight until death. No man has the right to take another man's freedom. And no army, no matter how big and powerful, dares to challenge the army squadrons of our Empire!"

The soldiers responded with a defiant shout of war. The deafening sound of their voices so united that the wind carried their divine cry to be heard throughout the entire desert of Pespire.

"Attack!" shouted King Alexis, and his heels spurred the belly of his horse.

"For the Empire! For the Empire!" the legions of the Royal Army chanted. As men charged forward on foot, they banged swords to their shields to challenge the enemy. King Alexis' horsemen carried spears at their sides, held ready to throw at the rapidly approaching enemy lines.

100 meters...

Each army closed in on the other.

50 meters...

In a matter of moments, preventing the impending massacre would be impossible.

Thousands of arrows arced into the air.

30 meters...

Soldiers took aim with their spears. Both of the armies quickened their steps.

King Alexis tightened the reigns of his horse and, with a flying leap over the front lines of the enemy, put himself right at its center.

Metal clashed against metal, swords slashed through flesh, spears pierced armor, and screams of death and moans of pain now replaced the courageous battle cries.

Bodies collapsed onto the ground, many of them dismembered. Others lay on the ground with arrows protruding from their chests.

King Alexis and his generals kept pushing their way through the enemy ranks, killing Jonaed's men left and right. Their plan was to get to the rear of the enemy lines, where King Jonaed remained—as always—behind his men. They would take the enemy king and slay him.

King Alexis knew that Jonaed's army would surrender if their king died, but the task would not be easy. As the ferocious battle continued, neither side seemed to be winning or losing.

Suddenly a trumpet sounded far away. A cloud of dust appeared on the left side and another moved in on the right. Jonaed's cavalry had arrived to join the fight.

Again the forces of the Empire were surprised. A rain of arrows fell on them, killing many more. The arrow of destiny, the one to fulfill the prophecy of the king's death, entered precisely between the armor plates shielding King Alexis and the left side of his chest. As another arrow pierced his abdomen, he fell from his horse.

In his last moment, the king was neither surprised nor afraid. He knew the Royal Army would not win. He knew he himself would die; it was his consequence for disobedience. He had given his all for his people, just as he resolved to do.

Seeing the king fall from his horse, a soldier yelled, "King Alexis is dead! The king is dead!"

General Geordano heard the soldier and instinctively ran to find his king lying on the ground. He lifted the limp and bloodied body onto his horse.

Swallowing his sadness, General Geordano mounted his horse and cried out, "Retreat! Retreat!"

General Levy, faintly hearing Geordano's words across the battlefield, repeated the cry for the soldiers of the Royal Army to retreat. He pushed his horse through the crowd of men who were trying their best to kill him. Some of the enemy's mounted soldiers galloped after him. General Levy kicked his horse forcefully, yelling, "Heyaa!" He needed to get out of there fast.

General Geordano shook the king as he retreated from Jonaed's men and pleaded, "My Lord, My Lord!"

The king didn't answer. He was dead.

Cradling King Alexis' body before him on his horse, General Geordano galloped and galloped, as fast as his steed could move, away from the raging battlefield. He struggled to grasp all that had happened. Disillusionment completely overtook him. His king, whom he had followed wholeheartedly and believed in so deeply, was gone. The anointed king was dead. There he was, lying on Geordano's horse, lifeless.

"We lost, Your Majesty," Geordano spoke the words aloud. "Our Empire is gone; it has fallen."

He thought of all he had lost in this battle: his beloved people, his home, and his place of refuge. So many pleasant memories passed through his mind of the children, the women, the streets of La Ataviada, the peace and the harmony that the people enjoyed. It was over now.

Then a startling realization came to him. The people of the Empire were now under the rule of King Jonaed. Their new king would think nothing of enslaving them.

Hurt and angry, he asked Jhaveh, "Have you abandoned us?"

Had his Creator left him, his people, and his Empire? The idea of ever taking back his beloved Empire seemed hopeless. Jonaed had gained far too much control.

All these thoughts closed in on him until Geordano cried bitterly.

The Mountains of Merendon! he thought as he approached them on his galloping horse. All the men would run this way into the mountains. They had nowhere else to go. He would wait to see if they came — of course they would — and then they could make a new plan.

Now victorious, Jonaed admired the scene before him. The Imperial Army was defeated. Now he only had to displace the cities of the West to conquer the entire Empire. Their resistance would be weak. But, just to make sure, he wanted specially trained warriors to take down La Ataviada.

He decided to divide his army into two, sending half his troops to the West to invade Parma Ilanga and taking the other half north with him toward La Ataviada.

As the battle came to its end, Jonaed saw the Royal Army's generals rapidly retreating on horseback. He thought it better not to waste time on them now, but to take care of this problem later.

General Geordano reached the Mountains of Merendon, careful that none of the enemy pursued him. At the foothills of the mountains, he waited for the arrival of any surviving Imperial soldiers who had eluded capture by Jonaed's troops.

Just as anticipated, Generals Troy and Levy and nearly 2,000 men on horseback soon arrived. Little by little, men on foot also assembled at the foot of the mountains. The total count of the remaining Royal Army was 7,000.

The men instinctively knew they had no kingdom where they could return. They were beaten men, and the battle's toll showed on their tired faces.

The 7,000 men who stood with General Geordano at the foot of the mountains had no idea what their future would hold. They had no inkling that they had been specially chosen by Jhaveh. One day they would fight with the Redeemer of the Empire.

When the sun set and General Geordano was sure all the surviving soldiers had arrived, they held a ceremony for the dead. They buried King Alexis by a small river at the foothills of the Mountains of Merendon.

To this day, his body remains in its original grave, next to a statue of his likeness that rises over 100 meters in height, his sword pointed valiantly toward La Ataviada.

After the ceremony concluded, General Geordano talked to his soldiers and said, "We will search for shelter in the mountains and wait for the precise moment to attack. We have lost the battle, and it would be suicide to try and fight against Jonaed's forces now. We will plan very precisely what to do next. And we will wait on our Creator for the timing of our victory."

Together they fled into the mountains and waited for the Lord.

Chapter VI

In La Ataviada everything was still and desolate. The only movement came from the sentinels walking the streets. Women and children remained locked in their homes. Foreign merchants had left, fearing for their lives. In the neglected and unkempt plazas, rubbish had accumulated. The sadness in the silence was palpable.

Thirty days had passed since King Alexis and his army marched to war. No news on how the army was faring had been reported to the city. Queen Megdany was desperate; not knowing anything was torture.

Meanwhile, General Melany walked the streets along with some of the other soldiers to post the order she had just issued:

THE DOORS OF THE CITY SHALL BE CLOSED AT ALL TIMES, DAY AND NIGHT. NO ONE IS ALLOWED OUTSIDE THE CITY FOR ANY REASON EXCEPT FOR AUTHORIZED SENTINELS.

General Melany was agile and stood taller than most women. Anyone could see she was exquisite—both in her heart and in her appearance. Her pure green eyes were the first thing you saw upon meeting her. In keeping with a general's appearance, each day she pulled her raven black tresses into a tight bun at the nape of her neck and neatly tucked the few wisps that escaped behind her ears. Though she never had children, General Melany considered the townspeople her own family and protected them very much like a mother would. Her spirit in battle was indomitable. In fact, she was so brave and fearless that she earned the nickname "Melany the Valiant."

After midnight the darkness grew very thick and did not fade as the hours passed. Clouds obstructed the light of the stars and the moon. A strong thunderstorm moved in and was pressing down on the city, about to unload its burden.

Swwoossshhhh! An arrow pierced the wind and struck the neck of a guard posted on the wall. Close by, another guard heard a low moan escape the fallen man's lips. Seeing his partner on the ground, the man ran quickly to his comrade, only to find he was already dead. The second guard was gripped with fear, but with no time for a reaction, another arrow silently found its target in his own heart.

A small group of Jonaed's trained assassins scaled the wall protected by the present darkness. The men advanced rapidly, killing Imperial sentinels all along the way, with only one of the guards upon the wall remaining undetected and alive. From the highest wall, one of Jonaed's assassins raised a torch and waved it left to right in an arcing motion, giving the signal for the army to attack.

Straightaway, the small and stealthy group of intruders moved to the next phase of their plan to assassinate Queen Megdany and Prince Eli. The man that delivered their two royal dead bodies to King Jonaed stood to receive a great reward, a kingdom of his own and the power to go with it.

A flash of lightening lit the sky followed by a loud boom of thunder, and large raindrops began to fall forcefully. On the horizon, an immense army stalked toward the city like a lion preying on its next unknowing victim. The lightning briefly illuminated the approaching threat.

"Alert! Alert!" the undetected Imperial sentinel now yelled from the wall's high tower.

Simultaneously, a series of fiery rocks catapulted from outside and crashed against the city's walls. Thousands of arrows shot into the air, searching for their human targets. The lightning and thunder intensified, giving the night an even greater sense of terror.

Surprised, the soldiers inside the fortress walls ran around as they desperately tried to orient themselves. The enemy's army was breaking down the walls of the city, and its arrows were raining down along with the deluge of heavy rain.

General Melany gave instructions to her officers and immediately ran from her post, straight to her horse. Leaping to mount it from behind, she headed for the palace at a full gallop.

The queen and prince... I must go to them! General Melany thought to herself.

Facing virtually no resistance, Jonaed's army moved quickly into the city where everything was now in total chaos. With each explosion, women screamed and children cried out for their fathers.

In her royal chamber, Queen Megdany cried uncontrollably. One of the catapulted rocks had smashed through the roof and blocked her secret route of escape. She could easily leave with her son through the door of her chamber, but she knew they would certainly be apprehended following that plan.

The queen piled furniture against the door of her chamber in an attempt to stop the assassins. She knew that it was no longer possible to get out safely with the young prince.

"What's going to happen?" she said through her sobs. *Perhaps the prince will die!* Doubt and foreboding dominated her thoughts. Queen Megdany already knew she herself would die, just as it had been foretold; she had no doubts about that. *But the prince is not supposed to die. How will he live if there's no way out?* She cried even louder as desperation completely consumed her.

The assassins located the queen's chambers, overtook the guards stationed outside her door, and killed them. The intruders removed the obstacles, entered her chamber, and found the unarmed queen in a corner standing helplessly before them. Without wasting any time, they approached her and Prince Eli to do as they were ordered.

Following the assassins, just a few seconds behind, General Melany arrived at the doors of the chamber, saw the royal guards lying dead, and prayed the queen was still alive.

Bursting into the room, Melany saw that she was too late. The slain queen lay on the floor. She turned to see an assassin with his sword lifted, ready to kill the boy.

Prince Eli shielded himself, expecting a blow from the evil man's sword, but General Melany acted without mercy or hesitation, just in time to slay the assassin and prevent the boy's murder.

With her sword still drawn and ready, Melany the Valiant grabbed Prince Eli by the arm, and tucked him protectively behind her.

The assassins lunged again and again, attempting to reach the prince with their swords, but General Melany did not let them get close enough to reach him. Anticipating their promised reward and consumed with their ambition, the assassins would do whatever they needed to kill the boy. They attacked relentlessly.

General Melany did not fail to protect Prince Eli. She bravely and skillfully pursued each assassin until they were all slain. As she plunged her sword into the last attacker, tears fell from her eyes. "Done! I did not fail you, My Lord." Turning around to face the prince, she added, "You're safe now, My Prince."

Prince Eli was in shock after witnessing the carnage. Tears poured down his face. He stood and stared into General Melany's eyes, completely and utterly vulnerable.

Melany paused to wipe his tears, quickly took the prince by the hand, and the two ran from the room. They passed through the salon, dodging the incoming catapulted rocks and crumbling roof. General Melany searched in all directions for a way out of the damaged palace.

"There, in the library, Prince! We can go out through the garden." She decided in an instant this route was the only choice. But as they ran into the garden, Jonaed's men, even more soldiers than Melany had faced in the queen's chamber, surrounded them.

Instinctively, General Melany again pulled the prince behind her back to protect him. She made a bold strike at one of the men, but he met her with exceptional strength, his sword clashing hard against hers and sending it flying from her hand.

She was disarmed. Shielding the prince with her arms, as he stayed tucked behind her, Melany slowly walked backwards.

With a thirst for death gleaming in his eyes, Jonaed's soldier raised his sword to kill them both.

At that critical moment, something marvelous happened.

A great light appeared in the night sky, illuminating the garden and blinding the assassins. Out of the light emerged a gigantic lion with enormous wings like those of an eagle. The lion roared ferociously.

Mounted on the lion's back was an angel, four meters tall and of very strong build. His clothes and the lion's fur shone like the light of the sun. On the angel's forehead was a pure golden diadem, and on his thigh he carried a sword — also made of pure gold.

He was Mickail, Commander of the Divine Army of Jhaveh. The fulfillment of the prophecy had come.

Leaning from his mount into the garden, Mickail grabbed Eli by the arm and lifted the prince to join him astride the lion. In the same instant, the lion fatally slashed Melany's attacker with his paw. Seconds later, he tore the other soldiers into pieces with his teeth.

Another group of Jonaed's men appeared in the garden and halted at a distance as they witnessed the carnage. They could clearly see how inferior they were in comparison to Mickail and his lion. Their deaths seemed assured, and they stood transfixed and terrified by what they saw.

General Melany was fascinated. She could not believe what she was seeing. As a young girl she grew up hearing stories of the Divine Warriors and the giant lions from Heaven, but never could she imagine she would actually see them in her lifetime. Yet, here she was standing in the presence of the most powerful warrior in the Universe who had just saved her life and the life of her prince.

Everything happened in an instant. The Divine Warrior and his mighty lion came and left in the blink of an eye. Prince Eli was now out of danger.

Returning to their purpose, Jonaed's soldiers apprehended General Melany and took her inside the battered palace.

Chapter VII

The prince held Mickail very tightly, crying. Unable to comprehend what had taken place in the palace, he only knew that his mother was dead.

Something really bad must have happened in his home, in his city, and in his father's kingdom.

Prince Eli did not know the reason for his rescue. He didn't understand why his father hadn't come for him instead of the angel. Neither had he any way of knowing that someday he would spread the True Worship to all corners of the earth. He couldn't foresee that even further in the future he would be the Redeemer to his people.

By morning, Mickail and Prince Eli arrived at the foothills of the White Mountains where the winged lion gently came to rest on firm ground. A flock of ravens also landed on the grass behind them.

"These mountains are home to the Yepoc Indians," Mickail said to the prince.

A flock of ravens settled on the ground nearby. Seeing them, Prince Eli pointed his finger and said, "I think those ravens are following us."

Mickail turned to see the birds that Eli had noticed. They started cawing and jumping, flapping their wings and puffing their feathers.

"Those evil creatures are messengers for Eduen," Mickail said. "They've been sent to find out where I am taking you."

"Eduen? Who's that?" the prince asked.

"Eduen is a warlock. He is servant to the Lord of Darkness."

"Why does he want to know about me?"

"Eli," Mickail said, gently rubbing the top of the prince's head, "if I explain it to you right now, you will not understand. And those creatures... Don't worry about them or Eduen. Evil cannot enter into these lands," Mickail assured the prince, pointing to the mountains. "Now let's be on our way."

As he looked into the lush forest, Prince Eli asked, "How are we going to get in there?"

The vegetation appeared so thick it seemed to the prince impossible to scale the mountains.

"Don't worry, Little Prince," Mickail said, turning to Eli with a smile on his face. "This land is holy. It has a special entrance. No man can enter without the approval of Jhaveh, but you were already approved before you were even born."

Mickail squatted and made a sound with his lips like the singing of a bird. A moment later, from between the bushes, a cenzonte appeared, known in the White

Mountains as the 'bird of a hundred songs.' The bird started to sing and twitch his head as if inviting them to enter the sacred mountains.

"Let's go," Mickail said and remounted.

As the lion followed the cenzonte, a secret path was revealed to them. Its entrance closed immediately behind them, and the raven messengers flew away, knowing they could not pass.

Soon, Mickail and the prince were no longer in the forest, but in a beautiful valley. The prince's eyes grew wide at the sight of many strange animals and new species of trees he'd never seen before.

Eventually they crossed four rivers and captured a panoramic view of the valley. "Amazing!" Eli said and began to ask questions as his curiosity grew. Mickail explained everything the boy asked him.

"These are the four rivers and each one has a name," said Mickail. "The first one over there is called Pishon; next is Gihon, Hiddekel, and the last one is the Euphrates."

Crossing the entire valley, they arrived at the foot-hills of a steep stone mountain. From its peak, a water-fall cascaded into a plentiful stream that fed the four rivers. Prince Eli's amazement grew as they traversed these beautiful lands.

"What's the name of this mountain and the river that comes out of that waterfall?" Eli asked.

"Well," Mickail began, "this is the place where everything began. Here Jhaveh created all life that exists on Earth even to this day. The river has a name like the others. However not everything Jhaveh has created is revealed to men. This river has a secret name. Divine

Warriors are prohibited from mentioning such secrets. We will continue by walking through this mountain. The other side is where the Yepoc Indian tribe lives. That is our destination."

"How can we walk through this mountain?" asked Eli, bewildered. "It's too steep! We should fly; it would be easier." He added, "The lion could take us to the other side."

"We cannot enter by flying, Prince Eli. What lies ahead of this mountain is sealed by the hand of Jhaveh from the heavens above to the earth below."

Bending to one knee, extending his wings and his arms to both sides, Mickail exclaimed, "Father, I humbly ask you to allow your servants to enter into your garden."

As his prayer concluded, a soft whispering wind whirled around them. Then a loud crash of thunder shook the ground and the mountain in front of them divided, revealing a secret pass that would take them to the other side. "This is the only way to enter," Mickail said. Prince Eli felt nervous and excited.

Walking through the mountain, the boy saw an array of dazzling lights reflecting off the walls. Running his hands against the wall, he realized what was catching the light. "Jewels! Mickail, there are jewels everywhere!"

Diamonds, sapphires, and rubies were imbedded in the mountain. Eli wanted to grab one but thought better. He remembered that this mountain was sealed from men. "Where is this passage going to take us?" asked the prince excitedly.

"This is the entry to Paradise," Mickail answered.

"What is Paradise?" asked the young prince.

"Paradise is the most exquisite, life-giving, and beautiful valley on Earth. It is also the garden where Jhaveh walks and the only land on Earth that can contain his power."

"Does Jhaveh live in Paradise?" asked the prince, intrigued.

"No," answered Mickail.

"Where does he live then?"

"He lives in the high mountains of the Third Heaven. No one can see him except for the Divine Warriors of highest rank."

"Have you seen him?" the Prince asked, brimming with curiosity.

"Yes, I have. I'm always very close to him."

"Really? What is his house like?"

"It's very big and spacious, and I don't think I can describe it to you in human words."

"Can you tell me what He looks like? Does He look like you?" the prince asked, pressing Mickail.

Mickail didn't answer.

They had reached the end of their walk. The mountains closed behind their backs, keeping the passage a secret from men. The mountains were perfectly still, seemingly immovable, and yet they had moved, had they not?

The other side of the passage was even more extravagant, with a bed of green grass and flowers covering the valley before them as far as the eye could see.

The waterfall and the four rivers could be seen from this side of the mountain too. Butterflies fluttered everywhere, the unique song of the cenzonte filled the air, and gazelles perked up their ears at the arrival of Mickail and the prince.

Paradise was more than enchanting. This was Heaven.

Eli felt the warm whisper of the wind tingling against his skin while gently surrounding him with the glorious perfume of flowers. Scanning the valley in wonder, his eyes came to rest on a lagoon filled with crystal-clear water right at its center.

The way the light of the sun kissed Paradise seemed to make it shine brighter than anywhere else he'd been on Earth. "What an amazing place!" exclaimed Prince Eli, with eyes wide open, unblinking.

Mickail turned to look at him and smiled. He didn't want to interrupt this moment for Eli with words. Mickail loved this place too.

"Is this where we are going to stay?"

"No," answered Mickail.

"Well, where are we going then? I want to be here!" Eli said.

Mickail moved close to the young boy, lowering himself to meet the prince's eyes. He pointed to the horizon and asked, "Can your eyes reach the mountains that are on the other side of the valley?"

"Yes," responded the prince, as he squinted and strained to see them. "It looks like they are very far away."

"We're going there," said Mickail. He picked up the reigns of the lion and scooted the prince a little further back. "Hold on tight," he added.

Airborne, Prince Eli continued to observe his surroundings. "Who lives here then?" the Prince asked.

"No one," answered Mickail. "This is The Paradise where all the stories of man began. Only Jhaveh has walked in this place."

"But didn't you say the Yepoc Indians live in this land?" the prince wondered aloud.

"Yepoc Indians are only the guardians of this place," responded Mickail. "They don't live here exactly. They live in the White Mountains on the other side of the valley. This land is holy, consecrated. They are not permitted to walk here. When the Yepoc cross the valley, they ride on the backs of giant hawks. You will see soon enough."

Prince Eli asked nothing else. He just let everything he had seen and all Mickail had said roll around in his young mind. He was content to take in the view.

At nine years of age, the prince grasped just how rare and pure this Paradise was. Nothing on Earth could compare to the life that reverberated in his every sense. He basked in the purity and goodness that he felt, letting it seep deep into his heart and soul. No one could see this place and be unchanged.

The lion descended, flapping his wings majestically. The Yepoc Indians gathered as they watched the sky. Once they saw Mickail, Commander of the Divine Squadrons, they exploded in joy and happiness, screaming with excitement. Then they all bowed their heads before him.

Jore, the chief of the Yepoc tribe, was a very gentle man and famous for his profound wisdom. Jore welcomed the two new arrivals, making reverence to Mickail.

"Do not incline yourself, Jore," said Mickail. "You and I are one and the same, servants of Jhaveh."

Prince Eli listened carefully to Mickail's words, thinking to himself, *Why is he calling himself a servant if he is so powerful? In my father's house, men make reverence to him as their king. I never heard him say that he was a servant. My father the king has authority over all men in his kingdom.* Eli tucked this thought away in his mind for later.

"Welcome, My Lord," said Jore. "I beg you, come into my house." Jore motioned with his hand for Mickail and the prince to enter his dwelling.

"After you, Chief Jore," said Mickail.

The children of the tribe came closer, 'oohing and ahhing,' and dancing around the lion. Prince Eli hung back to observe everything closely rather than follow the chief inside.

"I received knowledge of your visitation in my dreams," said Jore. "Jhaveh told me the meaning of your visit."

Noting that his young charge was out of earshot, Mickail responded softly, "This child is Prince Eli. He is the Chosen One of Jhaveh. He will take the True Worship to all corners of the earth."

Jore nodded with understanding.

"Jhaveh has ordered me to bring him to your tribe. You must protect him from the evil of the Blackfire." Mickail continued, "It is your duty to instruct him in all ways until he is ready to go back to his land."

"I will fulfill all that Jhaveh commanded," assured Jore.

Mickail took a golden horn from his belt and gave it to Jore. "This horn must be given to the prince on the day he leaves this place."

"It shall be done."

Mickail prepared to leave. "May the peace of Jhaveh be with you and all your family, Jore," said Mickail as he left the chief's dwelling.

Outside, Prince Eli waited for Mickail and faced him expectantly.

"Farewell, Prince Eli," Mickail said, caressing the young boy's chin with his finger. "One day you will become a very powerful king."

"Are you a king?" Prince Eli asked Mickail.

"No, I am not. I am only a servant."

"... But you are very powerful, right?" the prince asked.

Mickail bent down to look directly into the prince's eyes. "The greater your service, the greater your power. The greater your power, the greater your humility," said Mickail.

"Mickail, what do you mean?" Prince Eli asked, confused.

"One day you will understand all of this and more," said Mickail, smiling with reassurance. "You will understand that there is no greater glory for a man than to be a servant of Jhaveh."

"Are you going to leave me here?" asked the prince, feeling sad and insecure.

"Yes, Prince Eli, but if at any time you need me, all you have to do is call to me from your heart and I will come to you."

"Why do you have to leave then? Stay with me now."

"It is my duty," said Mickail, mounting his lion. "You must learn how to live and become a good man here in the place Jhaveh has chosen for you. Don't worry. I will always be by your side, even when you think I'm not."

With those words hanging in the air between them, Mickail flew away on his glorious lion and disappeared into the clouds.

Patypa, Jore's wife, came out of the cabin and hugged the prince.

Chapter VIII

"Sssshhh! Be quiet. Don't move," said Prince Eli, bringing his finger to his lips. "We have them right where we want them." Creeping slowly and stealthily, his body bent forward with his bow and arrow in hand, Eli tried to hide between the bushes.

Liam, Eli's hunting partner, was only a couple months older than he. Together they had lived as brothers under the same roof since Prince Eli came to the Yepoc tribe.

The two boys observed a herd of deer, careful not to make any sudden moves. Eli was closing in on the herd, and he had his eyes on the biggest deer to be his prized prey. Liam took a strategic running position, just in case the prince missed his shot. He would be ready.

But it was not necessary. The prince's arrow slashed through the air and landed in the deer's neck, killing him instantly.

"Aaahhhaaaa!!!" yelled Liam, excitedly running behind Eli.

Prince Eli, now sixteen, had become very handsome. His hair was soft and brown and his blue eyes were the color of the ocean. He was an excellent hunter, expert archer and javelin thrower. Eli had many abilities, and his heart was also kind and loving. His Papa Jore and his Mama Patypa had loved him generously and taught him well.

As Eli grew in wisdom, intelligence, and stature, there was no doubt that Jhaveh was with him. Whatever the prince purposed to do in his heart he accomplished.

Liam, his brother and the son of Jore and Patypa, was also a clever, bright, and handsome young man. Like all Yepoc Indians, his hair was coarse, black, and long, almost hanging to the middle of his back. His eyes were the color of amber and he was tall in stature, just like the prince. Liam was an expert marksman too. Unlike Eli, Liam was very outgoing and always looking for something to occupy himself.

After dressing the deer, the two young men prepared to move on.

"Three more days, brother!" said Liam. "Then we will be true warriors."

"Indeed, brother."

In the village, all young men who were successful in hunting would be celebrated by the people. The ceremony itself was very solemn, and all young men participating were required to bring an offering to Jhaveh. The offering was to be a true test of the young warrior. He must bring the offering that his heart demanded and knew would please Jhaveh. Jhaveh would then approve of each young man accordingly. Each would be blessed through the Prophet of the Mountain. The ceremony of approval consecrated the young men of the Yepoc tribe as warriors in both their physical and spiritual life. The blessing of Jhaveh would cover them.

Liam brought the horses from where they had been tethered during the hunt. Working together, they put the deer over the prince's horse and tied it securely. Both boys mounted Liam's horse and they rode down the mountain.

The brothers had been out of their dwelling since early morning and had been hunting all day. Rather than bother them in the least, it pleased Liam and Eli to bring meat home and provide food for their family, enough for many days. Besides that, they always loved the praise their father Jore gave them in front of all the other warriors of the tribe.

The brothers trotted slowly down the mountain, talking and making bets on exactly what their father would say when he saw them.

"'Oooh, children of mine, how proud I am of you two,'" Liam said, imitating his father and smiling. "I'm sure, that's what he is going to say."

The prince chuckled, affirming Liam's interpretation.

As they predicted, the wise Chief Jore, their father, wore a wide smile on his face as he stood at the front door of their home.

"Oh, children of mine! How proud I am of you two!" exclaimed Jore, raising his arms to Heaven as he approached his boys.

Liam turned to see Prince Eli's reaction to Jore's greeting and they both laughed in unison. In all truth, they loved this about their father. They knew he loved them very much, and in return they loved him profoundly. Their father was a gift to his family.

"Come, my sons," Jore continued. "Sit down at the table with your father and celebrate together the blessing that Jhaveh has brought to our house today."

Patypa came out of the kitchen, wiping her hands, and greeted her boys with a 'welcome home' hug. "Come eat, boys! We are waiting for you to have dinner."

Washing his hands, Eli looked at the scene before him. Patypa, Jore, Liam... all loved him, no question. Because of their love, Prince Eli had almost completely let go of his past life and the image of his mother lying dead in the palace right in front of him. And the doubts about what happened to his father also began to fade from his daily thoughts. But not totally forgotten, and when the memories haunted his dreams he would search for Mickail in his heart.

Mickail and his Yepoc family had all become his way of escape. They were the fountain where he replenished his love and confidence and discharged his fears and doubts.

Still, other times he would go outside the village to his very large, favorite rock. There he would sit, breathing in the quiet splendor of Paradise and releasing his sadness. Even though he knew Patypa, Jore, and Liam loved him as their own family, Eli knew he didn't belong there and longed to go back home.

"Eli...?" Jore said.

"Huh? Oh, sorry, father," Eli said, his train of thought coming back to his family.

"Let's pray," Jore said and continued. "Thanks we give to you, Powerful Creator of All Things. Bless this food you brought to our home today and bless our brothers. So be it."

The four of them opened their eyes, and after Jore clapped, everyone rubbed their hands together with anticipation and started to eat. Dinner was always delicious. Patypa was such a good cook.

"Mmm... Mama, this is so good!" Liam said.

"Right you are," Jore confirmed.

Between bites, Eli and Liam talked about their hunting excursion. Jore shared some decisions he had made and the fact that they needed to fix the roof of their home. Jore also urged them to make their best effort to please Jhaveh's heart with their offering on the day of the Ceremony of Approval. Dinner continued in this way. They made plans, laughed, and enjoyed each other's company.

Jhaveh had chosen Jore and Patypa to raise Eli. They were very special; they embodied in abundance the humility and kindness Eli needed.

Jore, aside from being wise, was a very eloquent man. He spoke with gentleness, acceptance and wit. Whether he was in the company of his sons or his friends, Jore would always find a way to fill the place with laughter and joy. He loved to tell stories, which were frequently repeated.

Patypa was also very special. She loved to serve others. She cooked with love. She was always ready to give a hug and ready to listen to anyone who came to her.

After dinner, the men went outside to prepare the deer for butchering the next day. Everyone went to bed happy and with a full stomach.

That night Prince Eli tossed and turned. The people of his empire filled his dreams.

A strong voice, like the sound of thunder, began talking to him. "Get up, Prince Eli! Listen! I am the Spirit, Creator of All Things. I am Jhaveh, Lord of your father and all of your elders. I have heard the pleading of my people. They live under the yoke of slavery in their very own land. My children suffer and have no rest. You are the one I have chosen to redeem them. In a short time you will leave this place you call home. You will go to the West, where you will live for half of a perfect time. All that you must learn is not yet complete."

The prince awoke from the dream, soaked with sweat and breathing heavily. Overcome with a clear call to action, Eli burst into tears, weeping loudly.

Jore and Patypa hurried to his room, surprised by his cries, and asked him what happened.

Still sobbing, he covered his face with both hands. "I had a horrible dream. I saw the people of my land suffering and a voice from Heaven that sounded like thunder told me that it was time for me to go back to my land and help them."

Jore listened carefully. The moment had finally arrived. He realized with sadness in his heart that the son he received as a gift from Jhaveh seven years before was now ready to leave. He loved the prince very much and for a moment his face fell. He might not see Eli again. Hearing the details of Eli's dream, he began to worry. The responsibility that awaited the prince was enormous. Jore also knew perfectly that as a father he had done what Mickail had asked of him.

At this realization, he reconsidered his worry and rejoiced in his soul. His boy was almost a man: smart, wise, and full of love for his brothers. Eli would soon be a true warrior approved by Jhaveh. He would be a powerful king.

Someday, he thought to himself, *I will be very proud for having educated such an honorable man.*

With a hug and kiss from Patypa and a few comforting words from Jore, Prince Eli calmed down and everyone went back to sleep.

The next morning Eli sat up in his bed, saying aloud, "What happened last night? My dream was so strange." The Prince's soul was still troubled; he had a profound feeling of being called to act and an overwhelming desire to go back to his people.

Flashes of his dream whirled around in his mind — tears, suffering, and the thunderous and commanding voice. "I have to go back," he said to himself aloud. "I have no other choice." He had to find peace for his soul. "But the voice said I wasn't ready. This doesn't make sense," he said to himself. "Why is it Jhaveh has troubled my soul this way and then tells me at the same time that I'm not ready? Why give me this revelation, if I can't do anything to free my people now?"

He dressed and ate breakfast in a daze and headed outside to walk the streets, eventually ending up outside of the village. There he brought both of his hands to his mouth, whistled like a bird, and waited a moment. A giant hawk appeared in the sky, answering his call, and touched down in front of him.

The enormous hawks were the only way the Yepoc had to cross the valley, since it was forbidden for them to set foot on its lush ground. Eli learned how to call them soon after he arrived in the care of Jore and Patypa.

Prince Eli mounted the hawk and flew toward the enormous rock that was his refuge. "I need to talk to Mickail. He'll help me understand what's happening," he thought out loud.

Prince Eli wondered why he had to wait for half of a perfect time to return to his father's kingdom. His people were suffering and he was the instrument Jhaveh would use to save them from slavery.

"I'm ready," he told Jhaveh, while flying through the air. "I don't need to learn anything else. They need me desperately!"

Landing on the rock, he let the hawk go on its way.

"Mickail!" he said. "Can you hear me? You told me to search for you in my heart when I needed you. I came to this place looking for you many times. You have never answered me."

A bright light slowly appeared in front of him, and Eli had to cover his face with his hands as it became increasingly blinding.

"I'm listening to you," said Mickail.

"Mickail, my friend! You're here!" Eli said happily. Seven years had passed since he last saw Mickail.

"Yes I am!" said Mickail, smiling. "I have always been near to you."

"Why is it then that you have never answered me?"

Mickail answered, "Before, you looked for me to rid you of your sadness. I am not a human to do such things. This time, you need answers."

"It's true. I'm very confused."

"Tell me. What confuses you?" Mickail asked, comforting the prince by putting his hand on Eli's shoulder.

"Well, last night I had a dream." Eli recalled what he had seen the night before and told the tale to Mickail. "These things I dreamt and this voice I heard. I don't understand why I have to wait to go back. Neither do I understand why I feel so much pain in my heart and desperation to help my people."

"You were born for this task, Prince Eli," said Mickail. "Your Creator Jhaveh has put a fire in your heart and burdened you for the souls lost in slavery."

The prince took a moment to respond.

"Yes, I do understand that much, but why does He disturb my soul with this dream and then tell me I'm not ready?"

"You must be patient," responded Mickail. "You still have so much to learn. The weight of your responsibility is not light."

"Yes, but why do I have to wait, if my people are suffering so much right now?"

"Jhaveh's designs are incomprehensible, even to us, the Divine Warriors. His ways may seem to be mysterious and even unjust at times, but they are always for your benefit. With patience and adversity, the earth transformed a piece of coal into a diamond. With patience, the potter molded a piece of clay into a beautiful vase. With patience, a seed of mustard germinates and grows into a tree for birds to take shelter. In the same way, with patience, Jhaveh forms the character of the man, little by little, living one day at a time.

A warrior can't be sent to war without training. Otherwise he will surely die. And that is what you are,

Prince Eli, a warrior for your people. Everything you go through makes you everything you need to be. A battle bigger than you lies ahead. Do not underestimate its significance."

"How will I know I'm ready?" Eli asked him.

"Don't hurry yourself," responded Mickail. "All things arrive at the precise time they must arrive. You will find all the answers to your questions. For today, be patient and wait on Jhaveh," Mickail said those final words and then disappeared.

Prince Eli stayed a little longer, sitting on the same faithful rock that listened to his words of sadness and caught all his tears, the rock that watched him grow. His rock was unmovable, always waiting for him and his dreams.

Submerged in thought, all the years of his childhood flooded his mind. He remembered how Mama Patypa wiped his tears every time he awoke after having the same troubled dream of his mother's death.

Mama Patypa cared for his wound whenever he skinned his knee. And whenever he asked about his father King Alexis, she always had a way of making his sadness disappear. She sat by his bed every night, whispering stories of adventure until he fell asleep.

He remembered his first hunting trip with his father Jore and Liam. Eli had beamed with pride as he walked home carrying a very large deer.

The prince would never forget his first season of giving and receiving with his family. Made by his father's hands, his first hunting bow.

He thought of all the summers he had with his brother Liam, running for hours through the forest, always looking for the wild horses. He recalled all they experienced together — the joy, the sadness, the games, and the disappointments. They were his family and now he had to leave them behind.

Sunset came and he decided it was time to go back to the village. With one shrill whistle, the giant hawk returned, and the prince soared home on his back.

When Eli arrived he learned that Liam had been searching for him. "Where have you been?" asked Liam, relieved to see him.

"At the rock that is my shelter," Eli answered.

"I'm worried, Eli," said Liam.

"Why?"

"Our parents are acting weird. They seem sad and I don't know why."

Purposely avoiding this very conversation, Prince Eli put his arm over Liam's shoulders. "Let's go," he said, and they walked back to the house together.

Dinner was silent. No one wanted to talk about Eli leaving.

Finally, Liam, who had no clue about the prince's impending departure, broke the silence. "Can someone tell me what's going on? Why is everybody sad today?"

Silence hung over all of them, ripe with expectation.

"Your brother has to leave," Jore responded at long last, after taking a bite.

"Leave? And go where?"

"He must return to the place he was born."

Liam thought for a second and looked at Eli. "I am going with you," he said. They both looked at each other for a second and then looked at their dad.

"The decision is not up to me," said Jore, trying really hard to concentrate on the meal and not on the conversation. "Besides, I don't want to lose both of my sons on the same day."

"He's my brother and I will protect him until he finds wherever it is he has to go, and then I'll come back," said Liam, trying to convince his father.

"In a couple of days you will officially become a warrior and a man. I cannot tell you what to do. But I will say this: If you go from these White Mountains, you will never be able to come back," said Jore, knowing very well this would not convince his son.

"I understand, Father, but I have lived for many years listening to Eli tell me about his life in the palace when he was a child. This has awakened my curiosity for knowing the world and other civilizations. Besides, if Eli leaves, I will be alone. I won't have anyone to hunt with or share my life with when that happens. Eli is my brother and if he leaves, my heart will be filled with sadness.

"Never has a Yepoc Indian left this land before," Jore said. "Jhaveh has put us in this place, generation after generation, to care for His garden. I am not the one that decides these things. We will consult Jhaveh about this matter," he added, "and if you truly want to go, and it is the will of Jhaveh, He will give you the desire of your heart."

Liam and Eli looked at each other and smiled with a sense of triumph and anticipation.

"However," added Jore, interrupting their joyful imaginings, "if it's not Jhaveh's will that you go with

Eli, then you will also have to accept his decision and be of good cheer."

"Yes, Father, I will."

"How do you feel, Son?" Mama Patypa asked Eli with a tender, maternal look in her eyes.

"Sad, Mama," responded Eli.

"The feeling you had in your dream must be very strong, huh?" asked Patypa.

"Yes, Mama. The suffering of my people is very compelling, but I'm also very sad knowing that I have to leave this place. You are my family."

"We will always be your family, Eli. Don't be sad or worried for us. We'll be fine here in these mountains, my son." Patypa said with a lump in her throat, more to convince herself than the prince.

"I know you'll be fine, but will I ever see you again?"

"We will always be in your heart and you will always be in ours. No matter how far from these mountains you may go, you will always be my son and I will always be your mother; Jhaveh has written that in Eternity. We are your parents and we love you," she said taking Jore's hand.

"Thank you, Mama," responded Eli.

"The time for you to confront your destiny has come!" exclaimed Jore. "I remember when Mickail brought you to our village. You were so little. You looked so vulnerable. I knew you would have to return to your kingdom someday. And that moment has finally come."

Eli didn't know what to say. He knew his papa spoke the truth. He moved the food around on his plate and said nothing more. He had much to think about.

No one felt like talking anymore. They all finished dinner quietly and spent the rest of the evening in their rooms.

Liam couldn't fall asleep that night. He was thinking about going with Eli. He recalled what the prince would say about the palace, "There were servants for everything, and we always wore embroidered clothes of rich colors, made of silk..."

He would talk about the majesty of La Ataviada, the merchants lined up at the port, the ocean, the great valleys, the desert, and the power of his father, the king. Liam loved when the Prince would recall his city, La Ataviada. Eli would get so caught up in the memories that he would forget he was in the forest with Liam.

And Eli talked about money, people using it to buy things from others. "What a strange idea," Liam thought to himself aloud. Money didn't exist among the Yepoc tribe. All these things and the ways of living in La Ataviada were totally unknown to Liam. His curiosity overwhelmed him at times.

A Yepoc Indian had never left the tribe to see the world and meet with sin like the rest of humanity. The Yepoc were destined to live a life of holiness, always dedicated to the worship of Jhaveh. Jhaveh protected them in the White Mountains, millennium after millennium, as they tended His garden.

The Yepoc aged slowly, it took many centuries for them to grow old. When they finally did get old, they were transported back to Heaven on a chariot pulled by horses of fire. From that moment on, they lived together with the Divine Warriors, becoming immortals and joining the Celestial Army. The Yepoc elders said they were a race of angels, especially loved by Jhaveh, who had not allowed their souls to be contaminated by sin. They were set apart and sent to Paradise to live a life of holiness.

The elders also told a story of another race of angels, who, at the beginning of Creation, joined sides with a powerful Divine Warrior who later became the evil Blackfire. Blackfire rebelled against the Creator and started a celestial war, converting one-third of the Divine Warriors into demons.

After that war, Jhaveh decided to convert every single Divine Warrior into a human being. He sent them to the world in the form of flesh and blood, weak and mortal, to live a life of suffering and temptation. They had to prove their loyalty to Jhaveh and also to be worthy enough to come back to Heaven.

Liam was awake for a long time thinking of all the stories he'd heard since he was a child and wondering if he would be joining Eli on his journey. Eventually, the stories faded into dreams as he drifted off to sleep.

Chapter IX

The next morning Liam went to the river, the one whose name is not given to men. The river was a holy place, and Liam was looking there for a particular precious stone.

This was the tradition of the Yepoc Indians, and Liam followed each step carefully. In order to make a petition, he must go to the unnamed river and find a precious stone, chosen by his heart, and clean it carefully. Above all, the seeker of the stone must believe Jhaveh would be pleased with the selection. Liam felt deeply certain that his chosen stone would be pleasing. Following the Yepoc custom, he then engraved his request into the stone.

The last step for Liam was to go to the temple in the mountain and present the stone on the Table of Petitions. Jhaveh would then answer through the prophet.

Very early in the morning after receiving permission from his father Jore, Liam went to the mountain where Osmer the Prophet lived. Every year, one of the prophets was called to serve at the temple to be in constant communion with Him. This year, Jhaveh had picked Osmer.

Liam arrived at the Temple of the Mountain, a beautiful place built by Yepoc Indians thousands of years before and hidden inside a rock on the side of the mountain. A trail of exactly 24 steps led to the entrance. The final step before the entrance was exactly 24 times the dimension of the other 23 steps.

At the front of the temple were twelve majestic columns sculpted from stone, six standing on each side of an enormous entry that arched at its highest point. In the entry, the temple floor was decorated with mosaics made of polished rock cut into pieces of varying dimensions and divided by small grooves. Further inside the temple was a large salon with no walls, its roof supported by twelve columns on the right and left sides of the temple. Twelve more columns were erected at the back of the salon. All together, there were 48 columns inside and outside the temple.

In the center of the open salon, a large solid rock table rose from the floor and sat perpendicular to the entry. This table was fully inscribed with angelic scriptures on each of its sides. On top of the table were three candelabras of pure gold with seven candles in each. Exactly seven meters behind the table was a curtain, made of fine white linen, covering the entrance to the Holy Place where the prophet presents offerings to Jhaveh.

The angelically inscribed table was called the Table of Petitions, and it was where the Yepoc Indians came when they had a request to make of Jhaveh.

With humility, Liam made a deep act of reverence to Jhaveh upon entering the room. He went to the Table of Petitions and kneeled with special care not to lift his head. Raising his arms slowly he put the precious stone on the table and prayed:

"Thank you, Father, for allowing me, your humble servant, to enter the living room of your house and present you my petition. I beg you to give me the desire of my heart."

Liam stood up, his head still lowered, and walked backwards with his face toward the table. He approached the exit to the temple, but before leaving, a voice stopped him.

"Liam, son of Jore," exclaimed Osmer the Prophet from the back of the room, "this is what Jhaveh says to you: 'I know your heart. It is noble like that of a warrior. Your petition is honorable. From the offering of your heart comes the blessing of your desire. Test yourself that you might please your Creator.'"

After the prophet spoke, Liam left the temple, still walking backwards with his head bowed as a sign of reverence to Jhaveh. Outside the temple, he mounted his horse and left. As he rode down the mountain, Liam thought about what the prophet said, "Test yourself..." *What can I do to truly test all that I am capable of?* Liam said to himself.

He thought about hunting one of the rams that lived in the highest part of the White Mountains. Getting to where the rams lived was a very difficult climb; it was steep and covered with rock. This made the rams hard to hunt, not to mention how powerful they were.

Liam recalled the words of his father: "If Jhaveh's answer is 'no,' then you must also accept it with joy in your heart."

"No matter what the answer is, I will hunt the most powerful ram of all; that will please Jhaveh," he said to himself.

On the other side of the village, Prince Eli watched his father's sheep. They provided wool to make winter clothes for his family and every now and then they were used for meat. With staff in hand and sitting under the shade of a lush tree, he began to daydream about what was going to happen when he had to go back home. What new things were waiting for him to learn? He desperately wanted the time to pass quickly. He wanted to be in La Ataviada, already fighting for his people, but he had no other choice than to wait.

Early in the morning on the day before the Ceremony of Approval, Liam went to the stable, took his horse, and departed with his bow and arrow, a spear, and supplies enough for three days of riding. He desired very much to accompany his brother Prince Eli on his journey.

Before leaving, his father gave him special instructions and, of course, told him at least twenty times, "Be careful, son." Liam knew his papa would love to go with him, but he couldn't. This was something Liam had to do without help from anyone. The offering for Jhaveh had to be something very personal. He had to give the best of himself until the ram was laid on the altar. Liam wasn't just bringing an offering, though. He also brought a petition. His offering had to be better than his petition. As deep and pure as the offering he was giving, so would be the blessing he received.

Eli was also thinking about his own offering. He wanted to bring an offering of peace and love because of his people. Eli chose from his herd a lamb with the most beautiful color and appearance, the best lamb for his Creator.

One day had passed since Liam left. In the village, the young men participating in the ceremony were getting ready for the day that would change their lives forever. Each one had a desire and an offering to give from the heart. Every young man would push himself to the limit. Many of the boys went to the mountains to hunt the animal their hearts demanded. Others already had their offering because they were shepherds or farmers.

The whole village was full of joy and anticipation. The ceremony had been a tradition for generations and was very special to all the members of the tribe. It was also very spiritual. The Prophet of the Mountain would participate. At this time of year, everyone in the Yepoc tribe not only drew closer together, but also drew closer to their Creator Jhaveh.

In his home, Chief Jore took from its place of safe-keeping and handed to Prince Eli the golden horn left for him by Mickail. Jore also gave him a leather bag he made to cover and carry the golden horn. Inside the leather bag, Jore also placed three smaller bags. In one were pieces of gold, in another diamonds, and, in the last one, precious stones.

"These things will be useful where you are going," said Jore, handing Eli the special bag.

Eli observed the bag. "The golden horn, what's it for?" Eli asked.

"I was not told the purpose of the horn," answered Jore, "but Jhaveh will let you know when it's time. Trust Him. Always trust Him. You belong to Him and His eyes are always on you. He will guide you on your journey."

After listening to his papa, the prince was reminded again just what he was leaving behind. He became very sad. "Why is it that I can't come back, Papa?" Eli asked.

Jore sighed sadly, wanting to avoid the answer. He wanted Eli to stay just as much as Eli wanted to stay. "Because this land is hidden from the eyes of all humans," Jore finally answered. Jore let the melancholy feelings flood his heart. "When you leave this place you will be exposed to the world and all its sins, and this is holy land. Sin cannot enter this land."

"Why does Jhaveh love this land so much?" asked the prince.

"Our elders gave us that answer," said Jore. "In Paradise Valley — also called The Gardens – is the place where Jhaveh was pleased to see all He had created in six days' time.

Eli loved the land of the Yepoc also, and he understood that to fulfill his destiny he was compelled to leave it behind.

Chapter X

The Ceremony of Approval had almost arrived.

Liam had been hunting the ram and, thus far, was unsuccessful at killing him. A couple of times he thought he had his prey directly in his sights, but he missed the target.

Standing behind a shoulder-height rock, Liam again searched the landscape for the ram. Ah, there he was, standing on the edge of a protruding rock not too far away.

The ram was strong and majestic. His chest puffed out defiantly as if making a challenge to the wind. *I am the leader of this herd,* the ram seemed to say.

Liam crept closer to his target, trying to keep just the right amount of distance. Thinking he had secured a sure shot, Liam pulled back the bowstring, aimed with precision, and held steady. Just before letting the arrow fly straight into the ram's heart, the ram instinctively sensed Liam's deadly intentions and moved, climbing deftly down the rock face.

Quickly, Liam moved into a new position. *Snap!* He stepped on a twig, no longer invisible. The noise alerted the ram and confirmed his self-protective instincts. Liam immediately crouched behind some bushes. But the ram didn't take any chances. He knew there was an intruder in his territory. Seeing Liam, the ram reacted instantly, positioning himself for an attack.

The ram charged straight toward Liam at full speed. Ready to overpower the enemy, the ram bowed his head so only his horns could be seen.

Liam also reacted quickly, dropping his bow to the ground. Arming himself with his spear, he stood his ground and steadied himself. Seconds before the charging animal reached him, Liam leapt over the ram, dodging the force of his attack. In the same instant, Liam plunged the spear into his back and shoved it all the way through the ram's heart.

The ram gave a moan of agony, and his front legs buckled as he skidded on the ground, plowing through the dry leaves and branches. Liam approached the animal with his hunting knife in hand to make sure the job was done. The ram was already dead.

Liam raised his arms to Heaven and gave a shout of triumph. He had done what he purposed in his heart. He hunted the ram, leader of the herd. "Jhaveh will be pleased with my offering," he said to himself.

Next, Liam gathered dry branches to erect an altar on the top of the mountain. Liam offered the blood of the ram to his Creator and then burned the carcass. The rising smoke was a pleasing fragrance to Jhaveh.

In the Yepoc village, the Ceremony of Acceptance began. Osmer the Prophet blessed all the young men that were accepted. Prince Eli was to be the final one.

When his turn came, the prophet stepped in front of him, waiting before the sacrificial altar. Eli took the lamb in his hands and slit its throat. As blood poured over the altar, he took the torch to make his burnt offering to Jhaveh. But before Eli could light the wood, the prophet interrupted him.

"Stop, Prince Eli! Step off the altar," commanded the prophet.

Eli obediently stepped back from the altar, when suddenly a plume of fire descended from Heaven and consumed the prince's offering. When the villagers saw the flames, they were amazed and struck with fear. The Yepoc reverently fell onto their knees with heads bowed.

A voice from Heaven sounded, "This is my Chosen One in whom I am pleased. This is the Redeemer of the Empire through whom all the prophecies will be accomplished." When the thunderous voice finished speaking these words, the flame died.

The prophet approached the prince and put his hand on the young man's forehead saying, "Here is what Jhaveh says to you, son of Alexis: 'Blessed are you among all men. To you I have given authority over all creatures that exist in all the earth. Go, be strong and brave. On your journey you will encounter many wolves, and it may seem that you are just like a lamb that has run off from the herd, but I am with you all the way to the end.'"

The prince was speechless. He couldn't quite wrap his mind around the meaning of these rapidly unfolding events. He knew that from this exact moment his childhood was over, and he had become a man. But the weight of Jhaveh's words still hung in the air before him, waiting for Eli to grasp their significance. Though he clearly heard the words, they didn't fully register. He thought to himself, *Did the Creator of the Universe, Jhaveh, just crown me as King?*

The next evening, Jore's family was at home, sitting around the table and eating. They discussed the events of the previous day's ceremony and the outcome of Liam's exciting ram hunt. When they heard a knock on the door, Jore rose from the table to see who was there.

"Blessed be your home, Jore," said Osmer the Prophet.

"Please enter the house of your servant, My Lord," said Jore, extending his arms in a welcoming invitation.

"I have been sent to visit your house. Your sons have found favor before Jhaveh," said the prophet, entering the family dwelling. "I have come to bless the steps that they must walk from this hour on."

Jore guided the prophet to the table. Everyone stood up when he approached.

"Come closer, Liam, and kneel," said Osmer the Prophet.

Liam came closer to Osmer and knelt. He put his hand on Liam's head and said, "You have pleased the heart of your Creator. The smoke from your offering ascended to Heaven and pleased Jhaveh. Your petition brought before Him has been answered. Go and accompany your brother on his journey."

After the prophet's words were spoken, Liam stood and reached for his brother, embracing him.

"Eli, son of Alexis, come closer and kneel," said the prophet.

The prince kneeled. Osmer took a small bottle of oil from his pocket, poured it over Prince Eli's head, and anointed him saying, "With this oil I crown you King and Lord over everything that exists on Earth. Everything that your lips or your hands bless here on Earth shall be blessed in Heaven. And everything that your lips or your hands condemn on Earth shall be condemned in Heaven. Go and leave this place. Your time here has come to an end. Your destiny is waiting by the door and the Universe is ready to take you where you must go."

And the Spirit of Jhaveh was in their midst.

After the words of the prophet were spoken, the prince stood.

"Leave tomorrow at sunrise and sail on a northwest course," continued Osmer. "Go to the city named Balfate and have faith. The Universe will guide you to your destiny. You must find Master Joed in the Forest of the Musicians. He has already received, in his dream, instructions about your arrival."

After the prophet left, everyone stared at each other without saying anything.

Liam tried to contain his excitement, because he knew his parents were sad, but he was going into the world with his best friend and brother. Together they would meet new people and see new places.

Prince Eli was thinking about his Yepoc family. He would never see them again. He would never share intimate family dinners again. He would never be able to listen to Papa Jore telling the same stories he'd heard a hundred times. And his Mama Patypa... he would never taste her food again. Eli would never enjoy the warmth of her loving arms. All of this he must leave behind in the morning.

He felt the sadness tugging at his heart and at the same time he thought of his dream. Instead of making him fearful of the future, the images from his dream gave him courage to go.

His heart calmed. He still had this last evening to enjoy with his parents. The four of them spent the time talking quietly together.

The lamps in the living room had burned most of their oil when the conversation finally dwindled.

"How long have we been talking?" Liam asked everyone.

"Well, I know it's been a long time," Patypa answered. "I'm going to say goodnight now, my boys. I love you, my beautiful sons. I will always love you," she said with tears in her eyes and hugged them one more time before walking off toward her bedroom.

Jore turned his attention to Liam.

"Son, I am so proud of you. You have become the finest warrior. Your heart and spirit are vibrant, strong and brave. You stand out among a thousand warriors. You carry my blood, you carry my heart, and you will always carry the love I have for you. I will think of you every day, and not a day will pass that I won't speak your name to Jhaveh. You are a blessing to me, Liam."

Liam had to admit that underneath all the excitement and adventure, he wanted to linger in the comfort of his parents' love and the home where he'd grown in their care.

"Papa, I promise I won't let you down. I will always be the best warrior for Jhaveh, for you and Mama, and for my brother."

With that, Liam trailed off to bed, but not before he turned around with a mischievous smile on his face and, pointing his finger at his brother, said, "Eli, I'll see you at sunrise."

"Hahaha!" Papa Jore and Eli both laughed.

Liam was truly genuine. In his heart lived a grand desire for adventure. Everything was possible and there was nothing he couldn't conquer. He loved his family in the same way, fiercely and with abandon. He would prove to be a companion worthy of his brother and future king.

The lamps were still burning, and now there were only two left: Papa Jore and Eli.

Eli knew his papa wanted to have a serious talk before going to bed; otherwise, he wouldn't be Jore. Neither would he be a good father. Eli was eager to hear all he had to say. He wouldn't be able to sleep anyway.

Jore began, "My son, great responsibility awaits you. Jhaveh has given me the blessing of raising you. I spent a long time asking Jhaveh what it is he wants me to share with you, father to son, before you leave.

The first is this: Dress yourself with humility and never forget to be simple in your love and merciful in the judgment of your people. Never let the orphan be abused. Don't let anyone die of hunger if you can help it. Neither should you allow the weak to be humiliated;

instead, defend them. Jhaveh has given you the power and courage of a warrior and a talent to serve. Always help your brother."

Prince Eli sat across from his papa, elbows propped on his knees, focused on what Jore was telling him, not losing a single word to tiredness or excitement.

"Don't let vanity creep into any corner of your life. Vanity is selfishness living in your heart, and it will do nothing but imprison you. Selfishness will lead you to a life where no one cares about you, and you will surely die alone. You are better off putting your hands and your heart to work faithfully for your brother, so you receive a blessing. Love your people. Be grateful for their souls and know that they are priceless to the Creator."

If Eli was a piece of parchment, his father's words were the ink bleeding into his soul.

"I love you, Papa."

"I love you, my son, Prince Eli."

With that they said goodnight and tried to fall asleep.

In the morning, more tears, more hugs, and more advice were exchanged. Prince Eli and Liam waved goodbye to Mama Patypa and Papa Jore, their hearts brimming with love.

Together they rode the hawk to the other side of Paradise Valley. Eli headed towards the mountains that had opened up for him seven years before, leading him to a new home.

Eli knew exactly what to do.

He dismounted the hawk, kneeled, and prayed, "Father, I beg you to allow Your servants to leave this garden."

The mountains revealed the secret passage out of the garden. They opened up again to witness the meeting of the prince and his destiny.

Liam and Eli had been walking for three days when they finally arrived in the port city named Vetulia. They walked the street full of merchants and bought adequate clothes with the little bit of gold their father had given them. They asked around for the ship that would take them to Balfate.

A stranger pointed them in the right direction. "You'll be a boardin' that ship there," the stranger said, "Cap'n Kaden's ship, La Lucerna." Eli and Liam looked at each other for a second, thinking they heard him snicker. Then they just shrugged their shoulders and walked toward the ship.

The brothers boarded La Lucerna and settled in for the ride. They were on course to the Northwest of the earth, and both were full of joy and enthusiasm. When they saw the ocean, their hearts swelled with dreams and curiosity. They imagined what they would discover and the adventures that were waiting for them.

Chapter XI

Now under the reign of King Jonaed, the great city of La Ataviada was no longer majestic, especially for the people who had lived their entire lives, generation after generation, behind its walls.

The women worked the fields all day under the strong hand of Jonaed's soldiers. The men were forced to lift heavy stones to build King Jonaed's altars.

The soldiers had strict orders that anyone caught running away should be put to death immediately, either by decapitation or hanging, in front of the others as an example. Fearing death, the people of La Ataviada did as they were told.

King Jonaed changed many things about the empire. His first act, after instituting slave labor, was to ban anything having to do with Jhaveh. Signs posted everywhere prohibited praying to, speaking about, or worshiping Jhaveh. What followed was the demolition of all temples built in the name of Jhaveh. In their place, Jonaed erected his own altars to the god of the Blackfire.

Following the destruction during the invasion of the city by Jonaed's forces, buildings at the port that connected La Ataviada to the rest of the world were repaired.

Some of the Imperial soldiers from Parma and Ilanga, along with their families, were able to run away before Jonaed's troops reached their cities. They also took refuge in the Mountains of Merendon with Alexis' generals.

Among the people that escaped to the mountains was a woman called Mercedes who respected the Divine Laws of Jhaveh. She was mother to a twelve year-old girl named Aledeny. Mercedes' husband, a soldier, died in battle.

Many years had passed for the people taking refuge in the Mountains of Merendon. A lot of the children had now grown into adults.

One of those children was Aledeny. She had become a beautiful young woman with dark skin, curly hair, and golden brown eyes. Because of her purity and humility, Jhaveh blessed Aledeny with a gift, the ability to speak of what was yet to come. She spent much of her time in prayer, listening for the Creator to bless her with messages of hope and relief concerning the refugees in the Mountains of Merendon.

One afternoon, while the displaced Imperial citizens gathered at the makeshift temple that had been erected in the mountains, Jhaveh called on Aledeny to give the people a message.

"Be strong, Ataviada! I have prepared a Redeemer for your children. He is the one with whom I am pleased, and I have crowned him with the right hand of my power as King and Lord over all creatures that exist in the fullness of the earth. Fill yourself with hope and wait on me, because truly I tell you that not one generation shall pass before you see the revenge of your Creator."

Aledeny's prophecy lifted their spirits, united the children of the Empire, and encouraged them to stand fast for their land. They would not abandon the lands that had been given to them by the hand of Jhaveh. The Empire carried their souls, their blood, and their history. They only had to wait until the day the Redeemer came back to fight for them.

The people had named General Geordano as their leader and, gathering what little belongings they had, took refuge further back in the mountains. It was also agreed that the refugees should not attack the enemy's army or the caravans of people who transit the Empire so that they would not be discovered.

General Geordano received news from his spies in La Ataviada that General Melany would be transported to the kingdom of Creta to a new prison King Jonaed ordered to be built. Although the refugees had made the decision not to attack Jonaed's legions, General Geordano thought it wise to ambush the caravan transporting General Melany in order to rescue her. The generals informed the people, and they also agreed Melany should be rescued.

General Levy came down from the mountains with a group of soldiers, armed with a plan to go to the Oasis of Kaukira to wait for the enemy caravan.

The next day, General Levy and his forces arrived at the desert of Pespire.

"That point is key, My General," said Officer Galel, pointing to the oasis on the map. "We know they will have to stop there to drink water and to rest."

General Levy said, "The Oasis of Kaukira is the only place they have to refill their water while en route to the East. According to our informants, they will arrive there tomorrow afternoon, but we will be positioned there tomorrow by sunrise. We have more than enough time to prepare for our attack."

The officer nodded in quiet agreement.

General Levy watched the sun sink into the horizon and gazed up at the sky to see the desert slowly being dressed in a beautiful gown of stars. He rejoiced to see his land again. The men trekked on through the night.

Before dawn of the next morning, the small band of Imperial soldiers arrived at the oasis and took position out of sight of Jonaed's expected guards. Hours passed, and exactly as they had been informed, the caravan transporting General Melany appeared in the distance surrounded by approximately 40 men on horseback. Anticipating the perfect moment to overtake the unsuspecting group, General Levy waited until all the thirsty men were occupied with drinking water, and then he gave the order to attack.

Jonaed's soldiers were outnumbered and surprised. The Imperial rebels easily gained control and took General Melany from her captors.

Officer Galel checked to see that all of Jonaed's men had been terminated without suffering; he noted one of them escaping on his horse. "After him!" Galel took a small escort with him to pursue the runaway, while all the others made their way back to the Mountains of Merendon to join the Imperial refugees hiding there.

General Levy and his men were triumphant as they returned to the mountains with General Melany. General Geordano came to greet them, and upon seeing Melany's condition, immediately ordered treatment for any wounds or sickness. Melany the Valiant was very weak and ill from being held in a dark cell for over seven years.

Four days later, Officer Galel and the rest of his platoon also returned to the Mountains of Merendon.

"Hail, My General!" exclaimed Galel.

"Welcome, Officer," responded General Geordano. "What news do you have for me? Did you apprehend the soldier who ran away from your ambush site?"

"We followed him for two days, My Lord," answered Galel, "but it was impossible for us to reach him. We were already getting too close to La Ataviada to safely continue. So I decided not to risk the men and to come back."

Worried, General Geordano sighed deeply, "We are in trouble," he said. "We're no longer safe in this place. We have to move immediately. The soldiers of King Jonaed will follow your trail and they will find our shelter, no doubt."

"They won't find us for awhile, My Lord," said Officer Galel. "We led them astray with a false trail heading in the opposite direction and covered our tracks all the way home."

"Well done, Officer. That will buy us some time," said General Geordano, somewhat relieved. "Give orders to have all the people meet here. We need to make a plan immediately."

"Understood, My Lord," responded officer Galel.

That afternoon, all the people gathered at the meeting place, murmuring and wearing worried expressions. They had no idea what was going on. General

Geordano had never before called them into a meeting with such urgency.

General Geordano climbed the highest rock and raised his hands to signal the start of the meeting and shouted:

"Citizens of the Empire! I am sad to inform you that our shelter is no longer safe. A caravan of soldiers is on their way to find us. They may arrive here in two or three days. We must leave this place immediately. I have called all of you here in order to tell you the plan I have in mind."

The crowd of 12,000 listened intently.

The general continued, "We will divide into three groups and again hide ourselves further into the mountains. This time, we will divide the soldiers and families equally and go in different directions. We will stay in constant contact by communication with messages sent on horseback. When the danger has passed, we will reunite."

The crowd did not know how to react to the news they were hearing.

"If you agree, please enlist yourself and your family into one of the groups. Bring only the belongings you can carry. Everything else, leave behind. We must hurry! The enemy draws closer to us with every passing minute."

As soon as General Geordano spoke, chaos ensued. All the refugees ran to their makeshift homes to gather their things. The people enlisted themselves into the three groups, as was ordered. A few hours later, the groups left their temporary refuge and disbursed, each going in a different direction.

Chapter XII

On the other side of the world, La Lucerna sailed on for 30 days and 30 nights without wavering, through both tranquil and turbulent waters.

At the moment, the ocean was a calm and enormous mirror reflecting the sky's red and yellow hues. As it slipped down below the horizon, the sun reminded the world of its beauty. The wind added its own splendor by softly caressing the waves and swaying them from one side to another in a jigsaw rhythm that gently lapped against the ship.

Prince Eli and Liam talked on the bow, admiring the magnificence of Creation. Suddenly the prince veered his line of sight to something mysterious on the ocean and abruptly abandoned his conversation with Liam.

Noticing his brother's curiosity, Liam asked, "Eli? Brother, what is it? What do you see?"

Prince Eli extended his arm to the water in the West. Liam shaded his eyes from the blazing sun and tried to find what the prince was pointing out to him in the water.

"I can't see anything," Liam said.

"You don't see that light approaching us?" asked the prince, still pointing to the ocean.

Liam leaned over the wall of the ship, straining his eyes.

"Where?"

"Here it comes," responded Eli. "Don't you see it? It's coming toward us, and it's getting bigger."

"I don't see it," repeated Liam.

"Get Captain Kaden!" exclaimed Eli.

Liam ran to look for the captain, who then followed Liam to the front of the boat to see what had so excited the prince. Eli was mesmerized, seemingly in a trance, his eyes fixed on whatever it was he had spotted in the water.

Captain Kaden strained his eyes to see what it was Eli thought he saw. The captain and Liam just scratched their heads, completely puzzled. They didn't understand what was happening.

Prince Eli was spellbound. His vision compelled him to focus exclusively on a raft with a small mast. On top of the mast was a very clear light that he couldn't describe. Eli didn't know if it was a hanging lamp or what, but he saw the light floating atop the mast.

Something or someone else was hovering over the raft, engaging Eli and hypnotizing him. As the raft approached, he could see that it was a beautiful young woman. Her long satin hair was the color of sunlight, and it waved with the wind like the waves of the ocean. Her eyes were green, very green, like the purest emeralds, and the smile on her face was even more beautiful than the entire Paradise Valley that Eli used to call home.

The prince was stunned. His eyes had never seen such beauty, and his heart beat strongly in his chest, begging to jump out. Eli could barely remain standing.

He ran from the bow to the stern, following the raft with his eyes still fastened to the young woman of the ocean. But then her raft disappeared, vanishing like a mirage in the desert.

It was only a moment in time. The ship moved toward the raft just long enough for him to meet Love.

Liam and Captain Kaden followed the entranced Eli along the deck of the ship and watched the trajectory of his eyes upon the ocean. Finally, the captain snapped his fingers in front of the prince's face. "Hey, Eli!" he shouted.

"Here, let me try," said Liam. He tried all sorts of tricks to get his brother's attention, but nothing worked.

"Has he lost his mind?" Captain Kaden asked Liam.

"Uuhh... Yeah, I think so. Did you see anything?"

"No," Captain Kaden answered, leaning back on the wall of the ship and throwing his arms in the air. "Only the heavens know."

Liam thought Eli's behavior was erratic and out of place. He was usually so composed and rational. The prince was not the type to see things no one else saw. Liam thought it best to wait and see if he snapped out of his trance on his own.

After a couple of minutes Liam asked the prince, "Hey, man, what's happening to you?"

"Huh, what?" responded Eli blankly, still gazing into the horizon.

"What's going on with you?" Liam asked again a little louder, trying to bring his brother out of this hypnotic trance.

Suddenly, Eli turned around and responded, "Don't tell me you didn't see her!"

"What are you talking about?" Liam said, more than a little exasperated.

"The girl on the raft!"

"Look, brother, I didn't see anything."

"The g-g-girl! The r-r-raft! Her e-e-eyes!" stuttered Eli, and adding, "You had to see it. How could you miss that?"

Liam lightened his mood. Watching his brother was actually kind of entertaining. "I think sailing is not for you, brother!" said Liam, giving Captain Kaden a sideways look and snickering a little.

Captain Kaden was intrigued with what Eli said.

Prince Eli noticed Captain Kaden's interest and approached him. "You saw it, didn't you?"

"No," the captain said emphatically, "I don't know what you're talking about."

"What? Are you telling me both of you were standing out here with me, but neither of you saw the girl on the raft? You're crazy!" the prince exclaimed wildly.

"Bah!" Liam burst out absurdly.

"No," said the captain, "I didn't see her, but..."

The captain paused, as if he knew something. He walked to the bow of the ship where Eli had been standing. He stared out at the horizon and asked, "What exactly did you see, boy?"

"I saw a beautiful girl on a raft," responded the prince.

"What did she look like?" asked the captain. "Describe her to me."

"Of course," said the prince. "She's very beautiful."

"You already told me that, boy," the captain said, smiling through his impatience.

Liam whistled, raised his eyebrows and smiled, mocking his brother.

Prince Eli stared at his brother for a second but ignored him and continued to describe what he had seen to the captain. "Well," said the prince, "she has green eyes like emeralds, and her hair is the color of the sun and wavy like the ocean. And..." as if to spite Liam, he added, "she's very, very beautiful."

Liam shook his head, still with a smile on his face, as if to say, *You're crazy, brother.*

The captain listened to Prince Eli's description and then walked off without a word of response. But the prince followed him and grabbed him by his arm. "Captain!" he demanded, "Aren't we going to do something about it?"

"About what?" asked the captain.

"The girl on the raft. Are we going to rescue her?" asked Eli, pointing with his thumb to the ocean behind his back.

"She is not a girl."

"What do you mean? I just saw her with my own eyes."

"I'm not sure what you think you saw," the captain said.

"What are you talking about? I don't understand," said Eli.

"Do you think you can let go of my arm?" Captain Kaden said, widening his eyes.

"Oh, sorry, Captain," said Eli, patting the man's arm apologetically.

The captain smoothed his shirt. "Thank you."

"Well?" the prince insisted on more information. "What do you think I saw?"

"I don't know..."

"What? What is it, Captain? If you know something, you have to tell me."

"There is a legend," the captain said quietly.

"A legend...?" asked the brothers in unison and their ears perked up at this word.

The captain looked to see how the sun was hiding itself behind the ocean. He glanced over at the prince, who was waiting expectantly to hear the legend.

Captain Kaden didn't say a word, and his silence intrigued Eli even more. "You see, boy," the captain finally continued, "between us sailors is a legend called the Princess of the Waters."

"How does it go?" Eli asked rapidly.

"Well... the legend describes her much like you did just now, but it's all *pah!* anyway, just a legend between sailors."

"But I think I saw this Princess of the Waters," said Eli.

"Well, if you say so. Now, I have more important things to do than talk with you about princesses and legends," with that said, Captain Kaden walked off to resume his duties.

But the prince didn't let him go so easily.

"Please tell me the legend. I know there is more of this story to tell," Eli said, pressing the Captain and grabbing him again by the arm.

The Captain spun around and nailed his eyes to Eli's hands gripping his arm.

"Oh, forgive me, Captain," the prince apologized as he let go for the second time.

"I hope grabbing me by the arm doesn't become a custom for you, boy!" snapped the captain.

"I promise it won't happen again."

"I hope not."

"Will you please tell us the legend?" asked the prince again, motioning with his hand toward a stack of wooden boxes on the floor where the captain could sit.

Captain Kaden glanced at the boxes and then noticed several sailors who were also now standing around and eavesdropping, intrigued to hear the legend too. After considering it for a few seconds, the captain agreed. He always loved an audience.

Liam, Eli, and a few more sailors crowded around to listen.

Captain Kaden began, "At the beginning of all times, Earth was only composed of water. The Holy Spirits living in Heaven, also called the Creators of the Universe, came down to Earth and flew over the waters, but they didn't find dry land. They decided to make the dry extensions of land over the waters. They called the waters 'seas' and they put limits to the water. The Spirits said to them, 'Until here you will reach, and beyond that you shall not pass.'

The Holy Spirits created animals, plants, sun and moon. They saw everything they had made was beautiful, but there were no men to care for Creation so they started a garden in the South of the earth and called it Paradise. There they created Man and Woman. Man was much like the Holy Spirits, and they talked freely to each other, face to face. The Spirits only gave one rule to Man: He must not eat the fruit of the tree planted at the center of the garden."

Liam and Eli looked at each other at the same time, smiling. They knew the captain was talking about home.

"Man did not listen and ate from the tree," continued the captain. "The Holy Spirits expelled Man and Woman from the garden for their disobedience. Man multiplied himself, and disobedience prevailed in all lands where men lived. Their rebellion rose to Heaven, even into the house of the Holy Sprits. So the Spirits decided to destroy all Creation on Earth with a flood, making the waters of the seas rise above the dry land, and saving only one family in a big ship called the ark.

When all the evil was wiped away from the earth, the Holy Spirits sent over the floodwaters an angel named Kodylynn to calm the waters of the sea. This angel is the Princess of the Waters. She returned the waters to their boundaries and uncovered the land. Kodylynn fell in love with the beauty of the earth and asked the Holy Spirits to allow her to stay and live on the earth. They gave her the desire of her heart along with her own kingdom. The legend says that in her kingdom the waters become angels."

The captain continued, "And since that time the Princess of the Waters sails the seas and all the waters of the earth to keep the waters in peace so they don't rise above their boundaries."

"According to the legend, only a very few men have seen the Princess of the Waters," added the Captain, looking right into Eli's eyes. "All men that have seen her were admirals and captains, men who went on to change the direction of humankind."

"When high ranking sailors traveling on the seas lost their direction, the Princess of the Waters, under the Holy Spirits' command, would guide these sailors to their final destinations to accomplish their missions. All who have seen her say she is beautiful, that her eyes are green like emeralds, and that her hair is like the best of the sun and the ocean together. That's the legend," finished Captain Kaden.

Everyone listening sat in silence, fascinated by the legend.

"If it's true what you say about seeing the Princess of the Waters, then you must be somebody very special, boy," said Captain Kaden, standing up.

The prince responded with a half-smile. All eyes were on him as the men considered what they'd just heard.

Then the captain and his sailors returned to their work, leaving Prince Eli and Liam alone.

"Is it true what you said?" Liam dared to ask. "Did you really see that Princess Kodylynn?"

"I guess I did," answered the prince, casting his sight once again to the water and recalling his vision.

Liam asked another question, but Eli didn't answer. He didn't even hear his brother. His mind was completely captivated by the memory of her beautiful smile and her beautiful green eyes. He would never forget her, and he had never experienced a feeling like that in his life.

His heart palpitated in a very strange way. It was like he was holding his heart in the palm of his hand, while it was still beating. But it was only for an instant.

He didn't know if he'd ever see her again. According to the legend, she was an angel, and not only that, but a powerful angel. He was only a young teenager with a very big mission on his shoulders. His destiny had nothing to do with the waters of the ocean.

What he did know, without a doubt, was that he would remember her for the rest of his life.

After awhile, Eli went to his cabin to sleep, but he couldn't close his eyes until very late that night, playing over and over in his mind the memory of the princess.

Liam had his own reasons for not being able to sleep. He lay awake thinking about his parents, but mostly about the numerous adventures that were waiting for him.

He recalled what the sailors told him about how to get where they were going once the ship docked, "You'll pass through a grand kingdom where the men call their governor 'Pharaoh.' When the pharaoh dies the people bury him in huge stone buildings dedicated to their gods. The buildings are in the shape of triangles with four equally inclined sides that meet together at a peak."

"Huge triangles and pharaohs," Liam said aloud to himself, trying to imagine what this might look like in real life.

They also told him about majestic cities like La Ataviada, which they called "the most beautiful city in the whole world." To reach it they had to sail north. They said whoever passed through that city wouldn't want to leave it ever again, because it was a powerful empire. Of course, they talked about the incomparable beauty of the women in La Ataviada. "La Ataviada is the Bride of Heaven," they said, "because of its prosperity and majesty."

No need to wonder for too long. I'll be seeing it with my own eyes soon enough, Liam said to himself, excitedly.

As Liam thought about all those things, his mind couldn't stop racing. He'd never been out of Paradise before. The only thing he had known through all his life so far was his family and the members of the Yepoc tribe. Now, he was galloping on an adventure that no other Yepoc Indian would ever live.

Chapter XIII

The days and nights passed slowly, with the ship sailing steadily until finally making landfall.

"Land ho!"

Yelling and whistling could be heard all over the ship. Everyone was excited to disembark. It had been 48 long days since leaving the port of Vetulia.

The port of Balfate would open its waiting arms to welcome the sailors with a warm dinner and a couple of beers. They only had two days to relax onshore before departing west to Jutiapa.

Liam and Eli knew the first thing they would do once they docked: take a bath at the port! With anticipation, they returned to their cabin to pack their belongings.

"So, what now, brother?" Liam asked, throwing a shirt in his bag.

"Well, I guess we stay in Balfate. I mean our whole trip is up to the Universe."

Universe? Eli thought while he packed. *What does the Universe have to do with my destiny?*

Then he remembered. The words of the prophet were clear: "Go to Balfate and have faith that the Universe will guide you to your destiny."

"Ready?" Asked Liam.

"Yep. Let's go." The brothers threw their bags and bows over their shoulders and went on deck to await their arrival in port.

When the ship had docked, they thanked Captain Kaden and his crew. "Thank you for the story," Liam said.

"Boy," the captain said, scrutinizing Eli, "if you see her once, you'll see her again."

Eli thought he saw something in the captain's eyes and said to himself, *He saw her too.*

"Keep that boy there in line, Liam," said Captain Kaden.

"Yes, Sir!"

With that, they said goodbye and parted ways.

The prince and Liam stepped off the ship and pushed their way out of the crowd gathered at the port.

"There are so many people!" Liam remarked.

Men from the surrounding area came looking for work, unloading the cargo and merchandise for the city. Children and homeless people asked for money.

Merchants yelled, "Hot food! Come and get it!"

Women walked around with flirtatious eyes and teasing smiles, making deals with sailors to sell pleasure for money. Still others were there pickpocketing, trying to make easy money.

Eli stopped at one of the food vendors selling bread.

"Well, brother, here we are," Liam said, with his wide eyes taking in everything around him.

"Yeah, it's good to be on solid ground," Eli said stuffing a piece of hot bread in his mouth and smiling because Liam's eyes were so busy.

"How odd! Look at the way these people dress, Eli."

"Liam, they're just clothes."

Just then Prince Eli remembered something his papa had said: "Trust Jhaveh, because all things belong to him, and his eyes are always watching you." Eli wondered why, just now, he recalled Jore's words so clearly. Hmmm... He felt for the leather bag that his father gave him and held it close to his body. As soon as they could, they got out of the pressing crowd and looked for the main street of the city.

Prince Eli saw an elderly woman sitting on the side of the street begging for money. Again the words of his papa came to him: "Don't let another die of hunger if you can help."

The prince walked over to the woman. Taking out his little leather bags, Eli pulled out a diamond and put it into the woman's outstretched hands.

The woman studied the diamond and marveled.

"Are you Eli, Son of Alexis?" she asked.

A raven cawed loudly from high up on a roof-top. For some reason the bird caught Eli's attention. The raven stared at him for only a second, cocking its head from side to side, and then flew away. *Weird,* Eli thought to himself and then drew his attention back to the old woman.

"Are you Eli, Son of King Alexis, My Lord?" the woman asked again.

Eli felt a mixture of amazement and shock. "I... I... am," he stammered.

The woman kneeled on the ground and rested her head on the back of the prince's hand, crying and giving thanks to her Creator.

Eli just stood there, not knowing how to react.

"Get up, woman," he whispered. "Don't do that."

The woman kept crying, but finally, after he begged her to get up, she calmed down and sat again on the dusty street.

"How do you know me?" asked the prince.

"The angel told me," she answered.

"Angel... what angel?" asked Eli, bewildered.

"You see, My Prince," she said, "many years ago my husband and I came to this city because we were running away from the war that King Jonaed declared on the Empire of the Seven Kingdoms. My husband, who was very old, died shortly after settling here. Since he died my life has fallen into disgrace.

"But one night, while I was praying to Jhaveh, I asked him not to take my life away without knowing the Redeemer of my people. He heard my begging and an angel appeared to me in my house telling me: 'Be full of joy, woman! Your prayers are heard. Jhaveh, Creator of All Things, has shown mercy to you. Truly I tell you, you will not die before knowing the Redeemer. He will come to you and take away your disgrace and poverty. When he comes, put into his hands this parchment.'"

"Then the angel delivered this," she said, revealing the parchment, "and afterwards, he disappeared. For a long time I have been waiting to deliver this to you. This is yours," she said handing the paper to him.

The prince looked at the rolled parchment, and didn't find anything extraordinary in its outer appearance. It looked like any common parchment. With slight indifference, he shrugged his shoulders and put it in his leather bag.

Eli was determined to continue on the course of his purpose. "Thank you. We are on a journey to find the Master of the Musicians. Do you know where we can find him?" he asked the old woman, hoping she might be able to point them in the right direction.

The woman looked at him, wanting to give her prince an answer. "No, My Lord, I do not know," she answered, "but don't worry. If Jhaveh gave this mission to you, the Universe will take charge and guide you to your destiny."

The Universe... there's that word again, he thought.

"What does the Universe have to do with this?" he asked the old woman.

"The Universe is the instrument that accomplishes all the desires of Jhaveh, My Lord," answered the woman.

The prince didn't say anything else.

"Then, do you know where we can pass the night?" he asked.

The woman pointed him to an inn down the street.

Once the brothers got to their room, Prince Eli took the old woman's gift from his bag, unrolled it and read these words:

"Go north to the Mountains of Taulabe. Search for the wise hermit of the mountain. When he asks where you are coming from, these words you shall answer: 'I come from the place where all the stories of men began.' When he hears these words he will guide you to the Forest of the Musicians. Save this parchment.

In it there is a hidden scripture you do not yet know how to read. In time your eyes will be opened and the secret will be revealed to you."

The prince looked down the rest of the page. It was blank.

Liam saw the confusion on Eli's face.

"How are we going to get there?" Liam asked.

"I don't know, but we will find out tomorrow," answered Eli. "Let's get some 'solid' rest," Eli said, making a joke about their first night not sleeping on a boat in a long time.

"Really? Is that all you have for a joke?" responded Liam, smiling and sinking under the covers. "Good night, Joker."

"Ha, ha, ha, ha!" laughed Eli.

Chapter XIV

The raven landed on the windowsill of the high tower at the royal palace, Eduen's cave.

"Hello, my little spy," Eduen said. "Finally, you have come back after many days. Let's see now, what news do you have for me?"

Eduen grabbed the raven and stared into the bird's eyes, penetrating them and digging into its remembered vision until he found the prince.

"Ah Haaaah! There you are." He could see Prince Eli talking to an old woman on the street. "You're in my territory now, little prince. You should be more careful. You never know who might be following you." He laughed out loud to himself. "Well done, bird."

Eduen had no conscience. He was motivated by evil and he enjoyed malice. He hated all that was pure and right. In fact, if his spirit caught wind of anything from the Universe that reeked of redemption, Eduen sought its destruction.

Eduen flew down the staircase to find Jonaed. "I have found the prince, My Lord King," he whispered in King Jonaed's ear with a soft and slow hissing voice.

"Where is he?" King Jonaed asked.

"Not far from here, My Lord, not far. I found him tonight in Balfate."

"Balfate!" spat the king. "Then what are you doing here? Go and bring him to me!"

"As you order, My Lord King," Eduen answered. Satisfied and pleased, he went back to his tower.

"Haahaa! No one can save you from me, Prince Eli, now that you've left your pretty little garden. This kingdom belongs to the Blackfire now. You will never redeem your people."

Eduen slaughtered the raven with a dagger and drank its blood. Then a sinister transformation began to take place. Black scales jutted out from beneath Eduen's skin and covered his entire body. Bones cracked in his neck and allowed it to stretch to at least ten times its normal length. His head bellied and bulged until it had taken an oblong shape, complete with a razor sharp mouthful of teeth. Claws jutted menacingly from his hands and feet.

Jumping to the ledge of the window, Eduen pushed off into the air just as a pair of riveted steel wings shot out from his back. The black dragon flew off to hunt and kill the prince.

Early the next morning, Liam and Eli bought two horses and supplies for their journey. When they asked for directions from the man who sold them the horses, he advised them to go north. Neither the horse salesman nor any others the young men asked could identify the wise hermit of the mountains. So they saddled up and rode nonetheless, trusting that the Universe would lead them to their destiny.

Their father Jore used to say, "The Universe leads men to their destiny more easily when they believe like children do — without doubts or questions."

After riding north for two days, the brothers came upon a traveling merchant on the road. They caught up with him and the prince asked, "Do you know the Hermit of the Mountain?"

"Yes. Why do you ask?" the merchant responded.

"We are trying to find him. Do you know where he lives?"

"Do you see that trail that forks to the left ahead of us? Follow it all the way to the top of the mountain. When you get there look for a tree that is separate from the others and is marked with two vertical lines connected by two downward diagonal lines. When you find the tree, wait there. The hermit will come to you."

"Thank you very much," said Liam.

Both of them waved goodbye to the merchant and then resumed their pace till they reached the trail, following it toward the mountainous ascent ahead.

The prince and Liam had been talking quietly for some time when a large shadow suddenly appeared, hovering over them. Startled, both boys looked up to see what was overhead.

A black dragon shrieked, piercing their ears. His size was easily five times that of their horses. His wings appeared scrawny and his scaly skin looked like it had been stretched too thinly over his bones, leaving bare patches all over.

The horses startled and bucked wildly, first throwing both Liam and Eli off their backs and then running away as fast as they could.

Hovering over Eli and Liam, the dragon sucked in a large gulp of air and blew a torrent of fire directly at the two boys on the ground. Liam and the prince rolled instinctively and barely missed getting singed by the dragon's flame.

"What is that?" Liam asked, jumping to his feet.

"Don't know," Eli answered with disbelief. "Looks like a dragon!"

"Looks like some kind of demon to me!" Liam panted breathlessly. They watched the flying creature to see what would happen next.

The dragon blew out another steady stream of fire, and it came close enough for them to feel its deadly heat.

"Ruuuunnn!" Eli yelled.

Dodging and darting as fast as possible to get away from the beast, Liam cried out to his brother, "Where are our bows?"

"On the horses!"

"And where are the horses?"

Frantically, Eli searched in all directions for their frightened mounts.

He looked up again just in time to see the dragon expose his claws, poised to trap them with knife-sharp precision. Eli grabbed his brother's arm and pulled him sideways with no time to spare.

"Uuuhhh... I don't think the horses are close by, brother," Eli said.

"How do you do that?" Liam said.

"Do what?"

"How do you always find the worst moment to make a joke?"

"I don't know," Eli said, with a silly oversized grin. "I guess that's one of my tal—"

"Jump behind that rock!" Liam shouted while pointing to a rock in the side of the hill.

Both of them accelerated their pace and leapt behind the rock, then ducked down to catch their breath.

The dragon passed over the hill, trying to see where they hid.

Behind the rock, the brothers found an entrance to a small cave, but before they could squeeze inside, the black dragon came back around, flying straight at their hiding place. Just before landing Eduen transformed himself into the disgusting image of the man that he was.

"Haaaaaa!" Eduen yelled, breathing on their faces. "Prince Eli. Hahahaha! You are in my hands now."

"Who are you?" Prince Eli asked, more than a little unsettled by the sight of Eduen.

"I am Eduen," he said confidently, taking a bow. "I'm going to tear you to pieces!" Leaping toward them, Eduen closed his eyes and instantly transformed himself back into the dragon.

"Haaaaaa!" he laughed in a shrill voice.

In the same moment, a clap of thunder sounded and a speeding ball of light came rocketing down from

Heaven, striking the earth in front of the cave and stirring up a storm of dust.

"Eeeeeeee!" the dragon shrieked and flew away immediately.

The two young men stood there with hearts pounding at a thousand beats per minute. Shielding their eyes and coughing, they waited for the dust to clear.

Before them was Mickail on one knee with his upper body bent over to the ground. His wings majestically extended toward Heaven, and his hand grasped a sword of purest gold that was stuck in the ground.

"Mickail?" the prince asked, "Is that you?!"

"Woah!" Liam said with astonishment.

Mickail stood up, "Yes, it is I, Prince Eli."

The boys approached him, and Eli asked, "Who was that, Mickail?"

"Eduen," Mickail answered, "an evil warlock and servant to the Blackfire. I must tell you, you're no longer protected by the Seal of Paradise. Be careful from now on, because Eduen will do everything within his power to stop you."

Mickail returned the gold sword to its scabbard and made a loud sharp whistle. The two horses returned obediently.

"Follow the path as you were told in order to arrive at the hermit's house," he said.

"Thank you, Mickail," Eli said.

"So long, Prince Eli and Liam, son of Jore," Mickail said and promptly began his ascent to Heaven.

"Goodbye, Mickail!" Prince Eli said, and they watched him until he was out of sight.

Liam was paralyzed. "Sooo..." Liam said.

"So... what?" Eli responded.

"That was Mickail?! I don't remember him being so..."

"Big and powerful?" Eli answered, finishing Liam's sentence.

"Exactly."

"I thought the same thing the first time I saw him seven years ago," said Eli, smiling.

The two brothers continued following their path as they kept out a cautious eye for Eduen.

Chapter XV

The trail ascended all the way to the mountain peak, just as the merchant predicted. When they arrived at the top of the mountain, Liam and the Prince spread out to look for the marked tree.

"It's here!" the prince called out to his brother.

Liam joined Eli. The two waited there as they were told.

The hours passed, and they decided to gather firewood to make camp for the night.

"Welcome to my lands," the hermit's voice surprised them from behind, and there he stood with bow and arrow at the ready.

Startled, the prince and Liam turned to face the man and, noting his bow and arrow, they slowly raised their hands.

"Who are you and what do you seek here?" the hermit asked gruffly.

"I am Eli, son of Alexis."

"And I am Liam, son of Jore."

"What are you seeking here in my lands?" asked the hermit again.

"We have been sent to your house by Jhaveh, My Lord," replied the prince.

The hermit observed them for a moment, "From where do you come?"

Eli remembered the instructions written on the parchment and responded, "We come from the place where all the stories of men began."

With that, the hermit's grimace disappeared. He lowered his weapon and said, "Follow me."

They walked together as the hermit led the young men to his house. Inside, he hung his bow and quiver on a nail.

His house was quiet, inviting, and well hidden from civilization. The hermit built his beautiful cabin close to a waterfall. His home was made of rustic logs slathered and sealed with tar. A hammock, most likely woven by the hermit, hung from the rafters of a patio with a beautiful landscape view of the ocean in the distance and the whole surrounding area.

"This is amazing! You can see the port of Balfate, the valley, and a bunch of villages from here," Liam said.

"I know," said the hermit, matter-of-factly, while stirring whatever he was cooking in a pot over the fire. The rising aroma tempted deliciously.

"You boys hungry?"

"Yes, Sir. Thank you," they said in unison.

The prince and Liam admired the life this hermit seemed to have. Up here it was tranquil, away from the noise of the people, away from the bustle of civilization, and away from the problems that keep men from truly living and destroy dreams without mercy.

"Now, how can I serve you?" he asked as he handed each of them a bowl of soup.

"You see, My Lord," the prince began, "we are pilgrims in route to the North. Our final destination is the beautiful city called La Ataviada, but at this time we are delayed by order of Jhaveh. We must stay in the Forest of the Musicians for three and one-half years to study at the feet of Master Joed. Through inevitable yet unexpected circumstances, we came upon a strange parchment from an angel delivered to us by the hands of a beggar woman at the port of Balfate. In that parchment your name was written, My Lord, as our guide to the place we seek, the Forest of Musicians. And this is why we are here, in your land and at the door of your house, because the Universe has brought us to you."

The hermit studied each of the young men while they told their story.

"If your orders came from the Creator like you say, then your journey to La Ataviada will be a long one," the hermit said.

Liam and Eli went on telling the hermit about all they had encountered since leaving Paradise and many of their stories from growing up together.

The hermit just sat and listened, not saying a word.

After some time, the hermit stopped them. "We should rest now. We will leave tomorrow at sunrise."

The hermit went to his room. Liam and Eli were left in the living room where the hermit had made accommodations for them.

Everyone drifted off to sleep peacefully.

Far away from the boys and their host, the warlock dragon Eduen flew in a disconnected and desperate manner till he entered his cave in the high tower. Collapsing on the floor, he transformed again into Eduen the man.

"Ahhhyeeee!" he yelled out in pain. Studying the damage in the mirror, he saw that his flesh had split open from his forehead, down his face, and all the way to his leg.

"Mickaaaaiiiiiilll!" he screamed angrily.

The hermit shared his plans as the trio rode along. "We will go further into the Mountains of Taulabe and then descend into the deserted Valley of Otoro. At its edge is a deep canyon, so deep you cannot see to the bottom. On the other side of the canyon, the valley extends further. Most travelers are not interested in passing through the Valley of Otoro. A story is told that the canyon will swallow up anyone who crosses it.

Even though the valley beyond appears to be a dry and arid desert, within it lies the Forest of the Musicians, hidden from the eyes of men."

Five days on horseback to the Valley of Otoro gave the young men more than enough time to get to know the hermit.

"Have you lived on that mountain your whole life?" Liam questioned him.

"No."

"Where are you from then?" asked Liam curiously.

"Same place as you are," answered the hermit. "I am the son of the first man created on Earth."

"I don't understand," said the prince, lifting one eyebrow above the other, still not quite believing what the hermit was saying.

"A very, long time ago I had a family," said the hermit, trying to explain himself, "my parents, my brother, and I, but I did something very bad. Jhaveh castigated me by giving me life without a limit to my days. I ran away from the house of my parents. I found a wife, had children, but all of them died and my life continued on. I decided then to be apart from everyone and live by myself. I could not bear to be hurt again in such a profound way, neither could I stand to hurt the heart of another. I have repented my entire life for what I have done."

"What is it you have done to receive such punishment from Jhaveh, and still punish yourself so mercilessly?" asked the prince.

"It would be shameful to me to tell you the answer. I will only say that Envy and Pride are very bad advisors."

"You haven't told us your name, Hermit," the prince said, changing the topic.

"That's right; what's your name?" asked Liam.

"I am Cain, son of Adam."

"I think... I have heard your name from stories the elders of my tribe tell us," Liam said, trying to recall accurately.

"And what about you? What is your origin?" asked Cain, averting any more questions about his life.

"I was born in the White Mountains that surround Paradise. I am the son of Chief Jore and my mother is Patypa. I belong to the tribe of the Yepoc Indians."

"And you?" asked the hermit, pointing to the prince.

"I am Prince Eli, son of Alexis, the former King of La Ataviada," Eli answered. "I am on the way back to my kingdom to help my people who suffer under the slavery of King Jonaed.

Cain rode in silence for a while.

"The weight you have on your shoulders is heavy, Prince Eli," Cain finally responded.

Eli didn't hear him. His mind had wandered somewhere else, and his eyes searched the sky.

Just talking about his kingdom and his people brought back his dream. As much as he tried to submerge the thoughts and feelings, hunger for his people and concern for their welfare consumed his heart. Eli was desperate. He wanted more than anything to have the power to prevail and to go straight to La Ataviada with no diversions and no stops. But even the most powerful king on the earth must submit himself to the will of Jhaveh, no matter how good his intentions are.

A shout from far away shook him out of his thoughts. "We will camp here tonight!" Liam said, almost yelling.

Eating around the fire that night, Cain watched how Liam and Eli acted around each other, brothers with a deep love that came from their souls. His heart sank, made heavy with sad memories of his own brother. Two sorrowful tears rolled down his cheeks. He turned his face, trying to hide his emotion, but Prince Eli saw his tears and came close to him, putting his hand on Cain's shoulder.

"What's going on, Cain?" Eli asked.

"Nothing is going on, boy. I'm fine," answered Cain, wiping his face.

"That's not true," said Eli. "I saw your tears a moment ago. Tell me, what is making you sad? Why does your heart hurt so much?"

"Well," said Cain, pausing with a sigh, "it's a long story."

"We're all ears," said the prince softly, looking at Liam and again at Cain. "Sometimes it's good to express your sadness. Tell us, and maybe we can help you."

Cain looked at the two brothers for a long time and said, "I've never told this story to anyone."

"Well, I guess it's time for you to get rid of that secret weighing you down," Liam said. "We're your friends. Let us help you by listening."

Cain rested his hands on his head and then rubbed his forehead with his fingers. He was unsure about telling the two young men what he'd held inside for so long.

They waited patiently without saying a word.

"Alright," said Cain finally letting out a deep breath. "A very long time ago when I was just a young man like both of you, I had a brother whom I loved with all my heart. One day we both brought an offering to Jhaveh, but I was petty and my heart was full of envy." The hermit paused for another long while.

"And then?" The prince, sitting beside Cain, gently prodded him to continue.

"Each of us brought a different offering to Jhaveh. I brought fruit and vegetables from my crops because I was a farmer, but I didn't pick the best of my harvest, so Jhaveh didn't like my offering. My brother, who was a shepherd, brought the most beautiful lamb from his flock and offered it to Jhaveh. He accepted my brother's offering with joy because my brother did the best to please Jhaveh. I felt rejected. Immediately my heart churned with hatred and envy. I went away from the presence of Jhaveh feeling angry. Later that afternoon, still seething with hate, I saw the skeleton of a large animal on the ground, took a bone from its head, and with this bone I struck my brother, taking his life."

Cain paused and sighed, releasing more than just his breath.

"For what I did, Jhaveh put this mark on my forehead and punished me, taking away the limit of my days."

Liam and Prince Eli had seen the mark already, but now they studied it curiously to grasp its meaning.

"With much time, I repented, asking for forgiveness. I have been asking for forgiveness every day since then, but Jhaveh doesn't hear my words. My sin is too big to forgive. I should have thought twice before doing what I did." Cain's voice softened and trailed off at his last words.

The Prince and Liam listened intently as Cain told his story.

"I have never been able to understand the purpose of my life, why Jhaveh still keeps me here," Cain continued. "Maybe Jhaveh has kept me alive for this very moment in time, and perhaps he knows that helping you will at last free my soul from punishment."

"My father Jore used to say 'everything created has a purpose in this life,'" said the prince.

"Your father is a wise man," Cain answered.

"I have a lot of sadness in my heart too," said the prince lowering his eyes and remembering what Cain said about his brother. So many times I've thought about my mother dying right in front of me. And when I think of my father—I don't even know what happened to him—and my people, I feel their suffering grip my soul."

"Be joyful for your pain, Prince Eli," said Cain, visibly more relaxed than before his story's telling. "Pain brings wisdom. And I tell you that truly wisdom is more valuable for men than all the treasures of the world together."

"You see, Prince Eli," Cain continued, "don't let the bad things that happened to you overshadow the goodness in your heart. Instead, allow them to transform you and make you a better man."

Cain continued advising them long into the night, and the young men listened carefully, taking to heart everything he said, until finally they all fell asleep.

On the evening of the fifth day Cain didn't stop to make camp.

"Why aren't we stopping to sleep tonight?" asked Liam.

"We must hurry," Cain answered. "We need to be at the edge of the valley tomorrow right when the sun rises."

"Why?" Liam asked.

"Only at the time of the second equinox of the earth is it possible to pass into the Forest of the Musicians," answered Cain. "Tomorrow is the equinox."

"What's going to happen tomorrow?" asked Liam, greatly intrigued.

"On the sunrise of the second equinox, when the sun peeks over the mountains, the first few seconds of sunlight will throw a beam against the water of the lagoon where the Forest of the Musicians lies. The sunbeam reflects off the water and creates a bridge of light over the cliff. This bridge is the only access you have to get into the forest."

"What do you mean by... 'you'?" Liam asked. "Aren't you coming with us?"

"No, I'm not coming with you. I'm only taking you to the portal."

"Why aren't you coming?" Liam insisted.

"I am not permitted to enter those lands," Cain replied.

"Then how do you know all these secrets if you've never gone into the forest?"

With a smile on his face, Cain turned to look at Liam. "I have been on this earth almost since its beginning, boy. I know this secret and many more. Believe me."

"Why aren't you allowed into the forest?" the prince asked.

"Because of my sin," answered Cain.

The prince suddenly pulled up on the reigns of his horse and stopped. "Do you believe in Jhaveh's forgiveness?" the prince asked.

"Yes, I do. I believe Jhaveh is merciful."

Eli maneuvered his horse in front of Cain's and raised his hand. "Stop your horse then!" commanded the prince. "Dismount and fall on your knees!"

Cain hesitated for a second, but after seeing how adamant Prince Eli was, he did as he was told.

Prince Eli approached Cain and put his hand on Cain's forehead.

"Do you repent of your sin, Cain, son of Adam?"

"Yes, I do," he said, and his voice cracked with emotion.

"Authority has been given to me over all creatures in the earth!" exclaimed the prince. "Whatever my mouth or my hands bless on Earth, will be blessed in Heaven. Whatever my mouth or hands release on Earth will be released in Heaven. By this authority and by this power vested in me, Jhaveh releases you from your punishment. Be blessed. Stand, Cain, son of Adam and be free!"

A flock of songbirds fluttered their wings and took flight from the trees, as if running from something dark that had suddenly escaped from Cain. There in the middle of the forest, at that very moment, Prince Eli used for the first time the authority Jhaveh had given him.

Relief washed over Cain. He breathed in deeply and let the blessing of freedom wash over his soul. The mark on his forehead disappeared, and he felt life returning to his body. From that minute on, his countenance was lifted.

"When you finish this journey you will be free to decide what to do," the prince said.

And the spirit of Jhaveh was there.

The night passed as they advanced down the mountains on their horses. Just before sunrise, they arrived at the Valley of Otoro.

"Hurry up!" urged Cain at a shout.

Prince Eli and Liam spurred their horses. The light of the sun appeared on the horizon, and riding faster and faster they approached the edge of the cliff. They could see the abyss that Cain had described.

"Don't be afraid!" shouted Cain. "Jump over the cliff!"

Feeling a little afraid, Liam and the prince hesitated, but only for a second. They grabbed the reigns of the horses very tightly and pulled their bodies close to their mounts. Then, cutting through the wind, they jumped over the emptiness.

They both stared at the other side of the cliff, a little desperate because all they could see was a deserted and dry land. But suddenly the dry land transformed into a large and lush lagoon. Where there had just been dust, now bushes appeared and green grass, and the lagoon gradually opened into a vast forest full of enormous trees that grew from the water. In the first instant, the lush vegetation seemed like a mirage, but soon it all became their present reality.

The first ray of light shot over the mountains from behind the forest and crashed against the water of the lagoon exactly when Liam and Eli jumped over the cliff. The light beam flew through the air like a shooting star, fixing itself just beneath the hooves of the horses and forming the bridge of light just as Cain predicted.

Liam and the prince looked down, curious to see this architectural spectacle of glorious light.

"Haahaa!" Liam shouted. "We're riding on a beam of light. Can you believe it?" If they had made their leap a second earlier they would've fallen into the emptiness of the canyon.

Still galloping, Eli turned back to see Cain on the other side of the cliff wearing a wide smile of gratitude. From Cain's perspective, the bridge vanished behind them and they disappeared into the nothingness, swallowed up by the mirage.

Chapter XVI

The forest glowed with vibrant shades and hues of green. The mountains stood majestically in the distance, and their image reflected off the smooth waters of the lagoon.

"Could you have imagined such a thing?" the prince whispered in awe. "Such a place of beauty hidden from the eyes of men?"

When they had been on the other side of the seemingly bottomless gorge, the brothers saw only a desert before them, dry and stale and devoid of life.

But here in the Forest of Musicians, pure crystal waters flowed. Exotic wildflowers reached for the sun. Butterflies flitted from blossom to blossom throughout the abundant foliage. Soft green grass carpeted the earth beneath the trees. The sky teemed with all types of birds, each humming and twittering its own beautiful melody. Pelicans swooped down to glide over the water. A gentle breeze blew, and the panoramic sunrise scene appeared as if the wind had brushed it with hues of purple, green, blue, and orange. The lagoon's waters reflected the multi-colored brilliance and retraced the beauty of Heaven above.

Liam and Eli felt as if they were awake within a dream.

The prince scanned the scene before him and made sure that his eyes savored everything. In the distance, he saw a hanging bridge. It was an odd bridge, because it began on the ground, crossed over the crystal clear water, and then turned into a spiral staircase, winding around one of the majestic trees and ascending until it disappeared between its soaring branches and the clouds in the sky.

Eli felt a breeze against his cheek, and a soft voice whispered in the wind, "Go to that bridge. Take the stairs where the musicians are waiting to welcome you. Hurry!"

The prince was startled by the voice, and he turned around, searching for his brother. *Hmmm... maybe it was Liam speaking*, he thought, but the voice did not belong to his brother. Liam was still hypnotized by the beauty of the forest and had not spoken a word.

The prince looked in all directions, trying to figure out who or what had spoken to him. Liam, a couple of feet away, didn't realize the prince had even heard a voice. Eli gave up when he couldn't see anyone else except for Liam and, shrugging his shoulders, decided to go to the bridge.

"Might as well. It's not like we have any other instructions," the prince said out loud, talking back to the unseen voice.

"Huh? What?" asked Liam. "What'd you say?"

"I said, 'Let's go to that bridge over there,'" Eli said, almost yelling.

"Alright, I heard you... no need to yell. Why are you mad?"

"I am not mad. I heard a voice and I am talking back to it. Didn't you hear it?"

"No, I did not. Weird things are happening to you since we left home; you're kind of scary lately," Liam said with a wink.

"Okay, whatever..."

They rode to the bridge, left their horses and began to ascend on foot. The higher they climbed, the stronger the wind blew. The branches of the trees swayed from one side to another, dancing to the currents of the wind like a soft lullaby.

At the top of the winding stairs, they discovered a stretch of land laid out before them. It rested lightly on the air and was connected to the trees by the branches. As they walked on the land, the young men found gardens, streets, and small communities of charming cabins. The people walking the streets were beautiful, pale, tall, and angelic. They dressed in long, clean, white tunics.

The prince and Liam walked slowly along the main street, taking in all their eyes could see. When the angelic people saw Liam and the prince walking by, they made a point to stop and greet them.

Suddenly, a little girl bounded up to them with a very cheery smile. "Hi, guys! How are you? I've been waiting for you for quite some time now. Welcome to the Forest of the Musicians!" she said with a curtsy, lifting the hem of her dress.

Prince Eli stared at her with his mouth wide open, but didn't respond.

"Follow me, please," said the little girl, offering her hands. "I will take you to Master Joed's house."

The prince and Liam didn't know how to respond. There were too many surprises all at once. They didn't even ask the little girl how she knew they were coming. They simply grabbed her soft little hands and followed her as if mesmerized.

"Oooohhh, I forgot! I'm so sorry. I was so excited to finally meet you that I didn't introduce myself. My name is Genesis. Now, which one of you is Prince Eli?" she said pointing her finger at each of them and moving in closely to inspect them. *A little too close,* they both thought.

Eli smiled, giving himself away.

"I understand. It's perfectly normal," said Genesis, nodding her head. "You're still in shock. The wind told me this would happen."

"The wind!" exclaimed the prince. Everything that had happened so far seemed unbelievable, but the wind talking was impossible, wasn't it? He remembered the voice that spoke to him at the lagoon.

"Yes, the wind," answered Genesis with exuberant confidence.

"You can't talk to the wind," Eli said. "It's impossible, is it not?"

"Oh, yes, I can."

"Nobody I know can talk to the wind."

"Well, I can."

"You can?" Eli asked with a note of sarcasm.

"Yes. I can."

"Mmmm. Not possible," smacking his lips together in disbelief.

"Yes, it is. Everything is possible in our forest," Genesis said, pointing to a cabin at the end of the street.

"Is that where we're going?" Liam asked.

"Yes, that's Master Joed's house," Genesis said.

Following her, they stepped up onto the front porch and waited as Genesis ran ahead of them into the living room.

"Master! Master!" she shouted wildly. "They're here. Liam and the prince—they're here!"

Liam and Eli, still at the doorway of the cabin, observed everything carefully and waited to be invited to enter. It was a very cozy place, clean and organized. At one end of the room was a fireplace, decorated with rustic colorful stones. They could hear the soft crackling of the fire devouring dry branches. On the right side of the fireplace were some musical instruments leaning against the wall. They recognized the harp and violin, but the others they had never seen before; they seemed very strange.

Suddenly the back door of the cabin creaked. A man entered, carrying a bundle of dry wood under his arm. He was a tall and skinny barrel-chested man wearing small square-framed glasses. The boys could see he was an older man, but his face was curiously younger in appearance. His hair and his beard were white and very long, contrasting with his dark olive skin. Youthfulness spilled over from his heart and into his large and lively, dark green eyes.

The man's tunic reached all the way to his ankles, where the laces of his sandals were tied tightly. His body was only slightly burdened by the load he carried. Raising his head a little, he saw the boys out of the corner of his eye, closed the back door with his heel and announced, "Welcome Prince Eli and Liam, Son of Jore. You arrived just in time. I've been preparing the fire for you to be comfortable." He paused to set down the logs.

"We've been anticipating your coming for many days," he continued, after catching his breath. "You can go on now, Genesis," he said, talking to the little girl. "Well done, thank you."

Joed straightened up and dusted off the wood chips stuck to his hands. "Come closer. Please, sit down next to the fireplace, boys. I imagine that you must be very tired from last night's journey, but I'm sure you also have many questions to ask." He waved them closer. "You look a little confused."

"How did you know we were coming today?" the prince questioned, settling himself into a chair.

"My dreams," answered the master nonchalantly, "and also the wind told me the moment you crossed the portal."

"The wind?" asked the prince, again trying to convince himself of something he thought impossible.

"Everyone in this forest has the ability to talk to the wind, Prince Eli," said Master Joed, leaning in toward Eli and raising his eyebrows.

The prince looked him straight in the eyes. "Hmmmm?"

"What is this place?" Liam asked, his eyes full of expectation.

"The Forest of Musicians," answered Master Joed. "This place is where all musicians called to the Celestial

Chorus of Jhaveh prepare. I am their teacher, Joed the Master Musician.

"I don't understand," said Liam confused.

"You see, boys, up there," Master Joed said, pointing to the sky, "is a celestial chorus of divine musicians who play perfectly the melodies of holiness that are pleasing to the ears of Jhaveh. As little heavenly beings they are sent here to learn all the musical arts. As they grow, they become masters. When they are ready, when they have grown in both music and wisdom, they are lifted back up to the heavenly sky to join the Chorus of Jhaveh. They live to play music that pleases their Creator."

Eli found all these things amazing, but what he couldn't accept was this idea of talking to the wind. It just didn't seem possible. You can't see the wind, you can't touch it, you don't know when it's coming or going or whether it is even 'there' at all... "So, how is it possible to talk to the wind?" he said, quite confounded and intrigued.

Master Joed pulled his chair closer to the boys. "It's like all the other things Jhaveh creates. Many of His creations are impossible to fathom, and there comes a point when you must accept what is by faith."

"Now, when Jhaveh created all things on Earth, he gave the wind a soul, a life. He did the same to the water, the light and the earth. These elements have the ability to talk to men. Men also had the ability to talk to the elements, but because of men's disobedience, the language they used became contaminated and the elements separated themselves from men. For a long time after going away, men tried to talk to the elements, but the elements refused to answer. Eventually, the idea of talking to the elements was forgotten and so was the language. This language became secret and forbidden and was not in written form. Here the elements talk to each other freely, because the Forest of the Musicians is far removed from the eyes of men and from their contamination." The master continued, "That's why you are here, Prince Eli, and also you, Liam, Son of Jore. It is necessary for both of you to understand the language of the elements."

Liam and Eli turned to look at each other.

"I'm sure you're asking, 'Why?'" said Master Joed, pointing his finger and tilting his head toward them. "Once you leave the frontiers of this forest, the elements no longer openly communicate as they do here. Instead, they talk to each other with words written in the wind. No one has witnessed this open communication before you two, except for Jhaveh and his Divine Warriors of highest rank.

"Why is it that the elements cannot talk to each other outside the forest?" Liam asked.

"Because they are visible. The eyes of men can see the water, the earth, and the light. This exposes their language to men and thus contaminates it. Only the wind is invisible and so cannot be tainted. The sun writes in the wind with light. The earth writes with the dust. The water writes with the rain. This is the way they communicate to each other outside the forest. The secret language must stay hidden from men, incorruptible."

"But, I have spoken too much," said Master Joed. "You must be tired. Your eyes look as if they haven't rested all night. Am I right?"

Liam and Prince Eli looked at each other drowsily, confirming the master's comment.

"I know that look," said Master Joed, chuckling as he rose from his chair. "Please rest well. A home and a bed have been prepared for the two of you. Someone will take you there in a moment. Have a good evening."

And with that, the master left the room.

Later, when the two boys were settled in their sleeping quarters, Prince Eli's mind spun restlessly, despite his physical exhaustion. In such a short period of time he had passed through so many changes, so many emotions, and for the first time he had felt love.

He needed a friend to talk to, someone that would give him advice, someone to put all these new happenings into perspective. How did this journey bring him closer to La Ataviada and to becoming a king? More importantly, how did any of these events bring him closer to saving his people?

He needed Mickail. Mickail always listened.

Eli got out of his bed, went outside and sat in a chair on the front porch, searching for Mickail in his heart. He felt a soft breeze caress his face.

"Mickail?" he said. "Are you there?"

"I am here, Prince Eli," answered the angel.

"You know me. I have so many things to say and questions to ask," said the prince, smiling.

"I know, Prince," said Mickail. "What's bothering you?"

"Well, everything that's happened to me in these past few days puzzles me, like coming to this forest to learn how to talk to the elements while my people suffer. Really, I don't understand the meaning behind learning these things."

"Returning to La Ataviada is just the beginning of your mission in this world. Everything you are learning—courage to fight as a warrior, wisdom and knowledge to rule your people, love and respect—is necessary for all that lies ahead of you. A man's wisdom begins with his fear of Jhaveh. The Universe will supply the tools you need to complete your destiny," answered Mickail. "If you want to understand how these circumstances fit into your future as king, you must learn wisdom. Wisdom begins with the fear of Jhaveh."

"Master Joed talked about these mysteries. Do you know them, Mickail?"

"What mysteries?"

"The language of the elements."

"Yes, I do. Why?"

"I guess I want to know if I can talk to you through the light, when I learn how to do it. Will you be able to read my messages?"

"I will always be by your side. I hear every single word you speak, and I am aware of every single thing you do," responded Mickail. "And yes, you will be able to communicate with me; the wind is everywhere. Good-" Mickail began.

"Mickail, when I was on the ship, I uh..." Eli interrupted.

"Yes," Mickail said, smiling knowingly.

"Did you see what I saw?"

"Yes... why?"

"Well, ummm..." Eli said, nervously scratching the back of his neck.

"Yessss?"

"Well... um... uh... I have this strange feeling."

"Okay? Do you want to talk about it?" Mickail said.

"You saw how beautiful she was, didn't you?" the prince asked.

"Actually, I know her."

"Really?"

"Yes, I do... so...?"

"Could you... Umm... No, you know what...? Forget about it. Let's save it for another time."

"Are you sure?" Mickail said, smiling again.

"Yeah, yeah, I'm sure. Goodbye, Mickail."

"Goodbye, Prince."

Chapter XVII

Sitting in a gazebo away from the villages and studying the secrets of the elements, Prince Eli felt the warm wind against his skin. Then he heard a soft voice, "Get up, Prince Eli! Get up!" He had been living in the Forest of the Musicians for three years now.

"Prince Eli, get up!"

"Is that you, Wind?" he asked.

"Yes, I am the wind," responded the voice.

Eli had been trying to learn to talk to the wind since being here, and so far without success. Now, out of nowhere and in an instant devoid of his effort, the wind spoke to him.

"Can you hear me?" asked the prince.

"Yes, I can," answered the wind. "Now, get up and go into the forest. Hurry! Something is waiting for you in the trees."

The prince got up quickly, forgetting his books on the bench, and followed where the wind directed him. Soon he reached an open space between the trees where the sunlight had no obstacles.

"Stop. Wait here," said the wind.

Suddenly, Prince Eli heard something rustle, and then a shadow flew over the clearing. He looked up and was completely amazed to see lions flying, like the ones Mickail rode sometimes. Without thinking twice, he followed them deep into the forest until they landed on the treetops. Eli stayed there watching them until sunset. One of the lions appeared to be the leader, and he held Prince Eli's attention, as if there were some type of connection between them.

"I'll come back tomorrow," Prince Eli said to the lions perched in the trees, and he walked back to retrieve his belongings from the gazebo.

Every afternoon the prince would escape his studies and go to the open space where he knew the lions would gather. He didn't tell anyone about these excursions except for Liam.

One day while lying on the ground staring up at the trees, Eli decided he'd spent enough time studying the lions, and he got up to leave. At that moment, the lion Eli had become attached to suddenly leapt in front of him.

The prince, startled, jumped back a few feet, and observed the lion just standing there for a minute. Eli stared into his eyes, not knowing how he would react, but the lion didn't make any dangerous moves.

Then the lion did something unexpected. He lowered himself onto his front legs and inclined his head, inviting the prince to climb on his back. Eli came closer and extended his hand to touch the lion's forehead. But before the prince was able to touch the animal, Eli's feet snapped a little branch on the ground and scared the lion, who jumped and flew away over the top of the trees.

The next afternoon, Prince Eli continued his daily routine of going to see the lions. Again, as he was leaving, the lion jumped right in front of him, giving Eli another chance to mount. This time Prince Eli made no mistakes; he reached out and brushed his hand against the lion, moving in closer very deliberately. The lion responded, slightly guarded, by stepping back a few steps. The prince made a gentle clicking sound with his tongue, "Tch, tch, tch, tch, tch," while slowly advancing toward the animal. The lion calmed down and gave the prince permission to caress his mane. He lowered his front legs, inviting the prince to get up on his shoulders. Softly and very carefully, the prince mounted the lion. Then the lion crouched down, pushed off the ground in a forceful leap, and flew into the air and out of the forest, heading straight toward the lagoon.

"Wooo hooo!" shouted the prince, looking at all the beauty below him as the wind softly brushed against his face.

Eli tucked himself in closer to the lion's body as he descended rapidly into a tailspin, with incredible speed. Just when the prince thought they would crash into the water, the lion pulled up and skimmed smoothly through the air just above the water. Eli reached down to touch the water. The lion planed over the water for a distance and then pulled up once again, heading west to the mountains behind the lagoon.

"This is unbelievable! Yeeaaaahhh!" the prince yelled. After having fun for a while, the lion returned to the clearing in the forest where they had met. They said goodbye to each other. Of course, now that he could fly on the lion, that's what Eli did every day from then on.

One day after class, Master Joed stopped Eli before he darted out of the classroom. "Prince Eli," the master called.

The prince whipped around and replied, "Master."

Joed looked at him for a second and said with a smile, "You have to give him a name, you know."

"A name? To whom?" answered Prince Eli.

"Come now, Prince Eli, you know of whom I speak: the lion, of course!"

"How'd you know about the lion?" Eli asked with surprise.

"Nothing is hidden from me in this forest, Prince Eli. I have knowledge of everything that happens here."

Prince Eli lifted his eyebrows, "Oh I didn't know, Master. Why do I have to give him a name? Does he not have a name already?" asked Eli.

"No, he doesn't. You must give him a name because he belongs to you," answered the master.

"Oh, I assumed he had one already."

"The lions are called the Guardians of Heaven, and only Divine Warriors ride these creatures. When the warriors hunt them, they give them a name and the two become partners for eternity. Now, Jhaveh has been pleased to give you a Guardian of Heaven. You must give him a name, because when you leave this place and go back to the world of men, he will only respond to you when you call him by the name you gave him here in the forest."

"Really?" Eli said, excitedly.

"Yes, really," said Master Joed.

"Okay. I will give him his name today. Thank you, Master," Eli said, running out of the classroom.

Master Joed stood waiting, and five seconds later Prince Eli came running back into the room.

"What do you mean 'leaving,' Master? Are we leaving?" asked Eli.

Master Joed smiled. "I don't know when yet, Prince Eli, but at the right time, Jhaveh will let me know and then I will let you know."

Prince Eli stood in silence for a minute. "Thank you, Master," he said and left the classroom, running off again in a hurry to see his lion.

Breathless, Eli entered the forest clearing and found the lion was already waiting for him. The prince approached and very carefully mounted the lion's shoulders. Eli leaned in close to his ear, and while caressing the lion's mane he whispered, "You will be named Rolsta from this day on."

The lion lifted his head and joyfully jumped into the air, flying toward the lagoon, their favorite place. But something was different today, something Eli couldn't explain was happening all around him.

Even the water in the lagoon seemed different, and while flying close to its surface, the prince noticed small droplets of water jumping as if they were somehow alive. The longer he looked, the more the droplets looked as if they were dancing to a melody he couldn't hear.

"What's going on? Rolsta, go higher!" Eli said.

As they pulled upward, Eli looked back down at the water and did a double take. The water from the lagoon jumped into the air and froze.

Feeling even more confused, Eli shouted, "Rolsta, go back!" He needed to figure out what was intriguing him. Getting closer to the surface again, there was something familiar about what he saw, and something was floating on the water.

"I've seen this before," Eli said to himself, trying to recall. "Who could be in the lagoon?"

Though he strained to focus his sight, Eli couldn't make out what it was. "Closer, Rolsta!"

In that instant, the waves climbed out of the water and took on the form of angels. First they flew toward him and set a barrier between Eli and whatever was in that water. Then the angels jolted him right off Rolsta's shoulders and sent him hurling into the water. Tumbling down toward its surface, Eli saw what had been floating in the water. His eyes opened wide in disbelief.

He'd wanted so badly to see her and now here she was, right in front of him—Princess Kodylynn, the beautiful Princess of the Waters who had stolen his heart three years before! She was looking right at Eli and hypnotizing him with her beautiful green eyes. The same feeling he had on the deck of the ship overtook him now. His heartfelt longings completely submerged anything rational inside of him. Eli, entirely captivated by Kodylynn, was not expecting the impact of the water. *Splash!*

After plunging into the water, Eli surfaced and took a deep breath. He looked in all directions in search of the princess, but she was gone, disappeared from his sight once again, without him having a chance to talk to her.

Rolsta came to the water's edge and dragged Eli, completely dazed, out of the water.

"I have to find her, Rolsta. I have to see her again." He wouldn't lose that hope. "Wait! Captain Kaden said it when I was on the ship—the water angels. He said that in her kingdom the waters become angels. This is where she lives!"

Eli was now convinced that he knew where to find her, but he still had to find a way to keep her in his presence long enough to talk to her.

Eli laughed out loud, joyously petting Rolsta, "All this time I've been here, and the princess was closer to me than I thought possible. So many times I could've seen her, and if I only knew how, I could talk to her... Wait! Genesis! She'll know how to get to her."

Eli mounted Rolsta and flew back to the wide clearing.

Genesis knew pretty much everything about the Forest of Musicians. She had been the source of so much helpful information already. Eli bade Rolsta goodbye and ran back to the village at breakneck speed to look for Genesis. Out of breath, he asked everyone he met along the way if they'd seen her.

"Genesis!" he yelled as he saw her approaching in the street. "I'm glad I found you."

"What's going on with you, Prince?" Genesis asked. "Why are you running around, desperately looking for me?"

Prince Eli bent over, hands on his knees, panting and wiping the sweat off his forehead.

"Well... what do you need?" said Genesis, raising her eyebrows.

"I need to know something," blurted out the prince, still bent over and gasping for air.

"What do you want to know?"

The prince took a moment to calm himself and then stood up, saying, "Three years ago, I left my house in the White Mountains. While sailing on the ship of Captain Kaden, I had a vision on the seas. I saw with my very own eyes an angel named Kodylynn. Captain Kaden spoke of a legend that named her the Princess of the Waters and said that she lived in a kingdom where the waters become angels. This kingdom was given to her by Jhaveh." The Prince's face dropped a little, "But after that day, I never heard of her or saw her again... until just this afternoon, when I was flying over the lagoon with Rolsta."

"Wait a minute. Who's Rolsta?" said Genesis, interrupting.

"Oh, Rolsta... He's one of the Guardians of Heaven that comes to the forest. We've become friends."

"A Guardian of the Heavens has become your friend?" Genesis asked. "I don't believe you."

"Yes, he has," continued the prince, "but please don't interrupt me. Anyhow, when I got close to the princess, these waves of water transformed into angels. They flew at me, at first trying to stop me, but I got thrown from Rolsta and fell into the water. That's when I saw her, Princess Kodylynn, between all the angels... Awww," he said, getting caught up in his own story. "She was looking straight at me with her beautiful green eyes," he added, losing his breath.

Genesis responded by furrowing her eyebrows in a quizzical expression, wondering to herself, *Hmmm, is he in love with this princess?*

"Tell me," pleaded the prince, clearing his throat, "is it here in the lagoon where the princess has her kingdom?"

"Yes," Genesis responded.

"Aaaaahhhh! Why didn't you tell me before?"

"Aaaaahhhh!" said Genesis, mocking Eli. "You never asked before!"

"How can I see her again? Tell me!" begged the prince.

"I don't know. But now you tell me: Are you in love with the princess?" Genesis asked, tilting her head to the side and narrowing her eyes at him.

"Be quiet, little girl!" said the prince, looking around and acting paranoid.

"Hee hee! The prince is in love," Genesis said, stumbling around and playfully clutching her chest.

The prince got down on his knee, meeting Genesis' eyes, and raised his finger to his lips. "Sssshhh, be quiet, Genesis. Someone will hear you!" he said in a loud whisper.

"Okay," said Genesis, disappointed, "but I was having so much fun." After a short pause she continued, "There is a way to talk to her," she said, sobering herself.

"How? When? Tell me!" demanded the prince excitedly.

"Calm down, calm down."

"Please don't make me wait any longer than I have to."

"It's actually quite easy. Send her a message with the wind."

"The wind?"

"Yes. The wind."

"You think the wind will give her my message? Can she hear the wind?"

"Of course, Prince," said Genesis. "The wind feels very delighted to carry a message sealed with LOVE! Hee hee! She's a very powerful angel, you know. She can talk to the wind, and she even knows the Secret Scripture."

"The wind, huh?" the prince said, standing up, rubbing his chin, and taking a few steps away from Genesis.

"How is it possible that I haven't seen her before in the lagoon?" he said, suddenly facing Genesis again.

"That's because she only comes to the lagoon once every seven years," said Genesis.

"Once? Every seven years? Are you sure?"

"Yes."

"That's a long time to wait for another accidental meeting," the prince said, throwing his hands up to the sky.

"Send her a message then."

"I guess I don't have another choice."

"That's the only way I know... *Lover*," Genesis whispered, laughing to herself.

"What? Did you just call me 'Lover'?"

"No, I did not. Must've been the wind," Genesis said, winking. Just then the wind, as if part of the game, blew a playful gust, making her hair fly all around her face.

"The wind, huh? Whatever. Thank you anyway, Genesis." And the prince walked off.

From that day on, he sent the princess a message through the wind every day.

Prince Eli never received an answer.

Chapter XVIII

One morning, while the prince was looking through his belongings, he came across the old leather bag that his father Jore had given to him back in Paradise. He dug his hand into the leather bag and pulled out the golden horn and the three smaller leather bags containing gold, diamonds, and other precious stones, and then shook out the remaining contents.

The parchment the old woman had given him fell onto the floor and rolled under the bed. Eli got down on his hands and knees to retrieve it. He picked it up and sat on the bed, setting the parchment next to his other things.

Suddenly he heard a voice saying, "Open the parchment."

"Uuuh," the prince drew in his breath, startled.

"Open the parchment. Your time has come," said the wind.

The prince opened it, and as he did, a laser-fine beam of light entered through the window and, landing on the parchment, inscribed onto the blank space a scripture that was unknown to the prince.

"That's bizarre," the prince said to himself. The scripture was moving and changing its form over the paper.

"What kind of scripture is this? What is its meaning?" he asked the wind.

"This is the key to the Secret Scripture, still hidden from men."

"But I don't understand it. I have never seen it before," said Eli.

"You'll understand it soon enough," said the wind. "This is only the key. When you can decipher this key, you will understand the messages written everywhere in the Universe: in the light, in the movement of the trees and the waves of the ocean, in the position of the stars and the moon, and in the singing of the birds and everything that exists in the Universe."

"How will I learn to understand it?"

"That is your duty, but I'll give you a clue: Everything you do in life has an effect on the Universe. This effect is the culmination of the scripture. In the same way, it is like being a sower of seeds," said the wind.

"First, can you tell me who writes the scripture?" asked Prince Eli.

"This scripture is written by all existing things," answered the wind. "It expresses its message in unseen ways with signs: when the trees or the waters move, when a shooting star crosses the firmament, when a bird sings... The scripture and parchment are the way to understand these signs. But it's not with your intelligence that you will understand the scripture. Instead it's with the reasoning of your heart. Always listen to the discerning of your heart to understand the nature of the Universe."

"I don't follow you."

"The scripture, Prince Eli, is in one way a fore-warning to men. Whatever feeling or action they make toward their brother affects the Universe. And the Universe sends a sign through the scripture back to men, showing what will come to their life because of their actions and emotions. In this way, the scripture is formed by the feelings and the deeds of men."

The prince made a face, showing his confusion. "Huh?"

"We're all part of the same Creation, Prince Eli," continued the wind. "The stars, the sun, the moon, the rocks, the water, mankind, you and I... But only the feelings and the actions of men can affect the Universe. For example, if a man's heart leads him to act with evil intent against his brother, he will reap evil, and the scripture will send the signs to bring misfortune into his life. But if a man acts with goodness towards his brother, the scripture will send the signs to bring good fortune to his life.

"I think I understand now," said the prince.

"Don't forget what I told you at the beginning," continued the wind. "You must understand spiritual sowing and reaping. If you bless your brother, you sow blessings, and then you will reap blessings. If you sow pain, you will reap pain. If you sow love, you will reap love. If you sow mercy, you will reap mercy. All you reap depends on the amount you have in your heart to give. Jhaveh has placed this spiritual law as the nature of existence," continued the wind. "All men reap according to the measure they have in their hearts to sow."

"Making sense of this mystery will give you the power to conceive the nature of man," said the wind and then was silent.

That same day in the afternoon, Master Joed sent for Eli to visit him.

"Good afternoon, Master," Eli said, entering Joed's cabin.

"Come inside, boy. I've been waiting for you." Master Joed was cleaning a violin. "Sit down for a minute, and then I want to take a walk with you through the forest. Are you still having those dreams about your people?"

"No, I haven't had one for a while."

"How's Rolsta?" Master Joed asked.

"He's good," the prince answered, forcing a smile.

"You've become good friends then."

"Yes, Master, there is a connection between Rolsta and me that can't be explained. I feel like he is a part of my soul."

"Let me tell you something, Son," said Master Joed. "Your friendship will last forever. Jhaveh has ordered Rolsta to be by your side until the last day of your life.

"Really? How do you know that?"

"Oh, I know many things Eli," said Master Joed. He rose from his chair, set the violin against the wall, and dusted off his hands.

"Ready?"

They left the house and walked through the gardens behind it, taking a little path that led to the forest.

"This morning I talked with your brother Liam. He's actually become quite an excellent musician. He's also learned the words of the wind perfectly."

"What did you guys talk about?" asked Prince Eli.

"The time for you to leave has come," said Master Joed, his voice wavering with sadness. "You might never return."

Prince Eli didn't respond.

"It's necessary I talk to you in the same manner I talked with Liam," said Master Joed.

"I hear you, Master," said the prince, inclining himself slightly.

Master Joed stopped walking and stood staring into the prince's eyes and thinking of the sixteen year-old boys he met three years before. He regarded the prince and Liam very much as his beloved sons.

Facing Eli, Joed put both hands on his shoulders. "Jhaveh has given you the biggest responsibility, son of mine. Your calling is to spread the True Worship to all corners of the earth. You must be very brave to fight for your brothers. Be wise in judging them. Be merciful to love them the way they are expecting to be loved. You have been blessed to be in a season where you feel Jhaveh is with you constantly, but when you leave the Forest of Musicians times will come when you will think Jhaveh has abandoned you. But it's not like that; those will be times of learning. As I'm sure you have heard many times, there are still things hidden from your heart that you need to learn."

"Why are you telling me all of this, Master?" asked the prince. "The way you're talking makes it seem like something bad is going to happen to me."

"I don't know what's going to happen to you and your brother when you leave the forest," responded Master Joed, "but Jhaveh put these words on my lips for you to hear."

"When do we leave?"

"Tomorrow."

"Tomorrow? Why so soon?" asked the prince with surprise.

"Your time here is done. You learned all you had to learn. You heard all you needed to hear."

"But I still don't know how to read and write the Secret Scripture."

"The scripture you will learn to read and write in the world of men. The secret has been revealed to you through the parchment. The parchment is the key."

"How will I learn if you're not there to teach me?"

"This is something you must learn by yourself," answered the master. "Apply the love and the wisdom of the Universe to your heart."

"Will we be able to come back someday, Master?"

"Cain showed you how to get here," answered Master Joed. "If it's your desire and the desire of Jhaveh, we will always be here."

"Thank you for being like a father to Liam and to me, Master Joed," said the prince. "We will never forget what we learned from you. We will always hold you in our hearts with affection."

"Let me tell you one last thing," continued Master Joed, putting his finger in Eli's face for emphasis. "Don't put limits on your dreams. Use everything you've been given as you search and accomplish your purpose. In this way you will affect the Universe in your favor. The Universe is no more than an infinite warehouse where all the dreams of men sit on shelves. But very few valiant men claim what belongs to them. Be you one of those valiant men! Fight with courage and with vigor until you get there. Don't hesitate when circumstances seem adverse. The will of Jhaveh is for you to have everything you purpose to have in this life if it's good for your life."

"Do not misunderstand this to be self-indulgence. Whatever may seem a pain to you adds virtue to your temperament in the eyes of Jhaveh. And whatever may seem to be unnecessary to Him is essential. Finally, when you get to the end of a trial, all that you thought was painful or unnecessary you will know was actually the tool that permitted you to reach the dreams you had when you first began."

Prince Eli listened carefully to the advice of his master.

"Rolsta has been given to you by Jhaveh. Take him with you."

They turned and walked back to the village, and when they arrived, the prince when straight to his cabin to pack all of his belongings.

Liam already had everything in order.

The next day all musicians of the forest gathered in the cabin of Master Joed to say goodbye to Liam and Eli. Some brought a little farewell gift. Master Joed brought Liam a beautiful figurine in the shape of a harp made out of pure gold to recognize his dedication and accomplishment to learn music. For Eli, Master Joed brought a harness and saddle for Rolsta made of a material that shone like the sun, which made Prince Eli very happy.

"How will we get out of the forest?" the prince asked Master Joed.

"The wind will guide you."

"We will miss you a lot," said the prince.

"We will miss you too," said Master Joed. "And if one day you want to come back, you already know the way."

"It's settled then," said Liam. "One day we will come back, Master."

Genesis approached the young men with tears streaming down her face. She gave them both a farewell hug and then, just for Prince Eli, she gave a playful punch to the stomach.

"I'm going to miss you, Prince," she said. "I won't have anyone to talk to anymore, no one to make jokes with."

The prince smiled widely.

"I'll only ask that you never forget me," said Genesis. "If one day you meet Princess Kodylynn, tell her — I am her fan."

"I am going to miss you too, you little menace. I hope one day I can give the princess your message," Prince Eli answered with a smile, a nod, and a wink. "Oh and don't worry, I will never forget you. You can be sure of that."

A while after everyone had a chance to say good-bye, Master Joed came close to the two young men.

"Listen to my words, boys, and never forget them. All men have great talents given to them by Jhaveh. Most men are afraid to exercise them. The worries and the experiences of their lives slowly separate them from their talents, until they forget what Jhaveh has given them. Do not become those men.

"Listen! The musician can move the earth with his music. He can obligate the wind to bend notes so beautiful and powerful that they would delight the very heavens. He can create melodies with the noise of the waves, harmonies with the trail of a shooting star and the sound of nature making a rhythm.

"The writer can find all the words written in the wind, in the light, in the invisible feelings, and in all things he wants. He can write sentences in the nothingness using only the pen and ink of his imagination. He can create paragraphs with beams of sunlight. He can adorn the moon, the stars and whatever he wants in the Universe with the letters he writes.

"There is nothing more powerful than the conviction of a man when he knows nothing can stop him. When this happens, the Universe gives birth to the necessary tools for the next chapter in his life. You, Liam, are the musician. Eli, you are the writer."

The two brothers listened to the master, cherishing everything he said in their hearts.

Finally the prince shouted for Rolsta, who appeared a moment later. After a warm hug from Master Joed, the two mounted Rolsta and flew off into the sky.

Chapter XIX

King Alexis' people continued to suffer, but they held onto each other, knitted together by the hope that a Redeemer would come and also by the common belief in Jhaveh.

News spread among them, throughout the Empire of the Seven Kingdoms, that the generals of King Alexis' army had been hiding in the Mountains of Merendon. Those that could manage it somehow escaped from their lives of slavery, finding their way into the mountains to join the generals in hiding. Some sent their sons to add number to the Imperial Rebel Army. Sometimes whole families were sent by their compatriots, because they suffered more than the others. Still, those who escaped were few in number.

General Geordano's rebel army increased to 12,000 men. He divided them into four squadrons of 3,000 soldiers, commanded by the four generals of the Imperial Army. The rebels and refugees took shelter on the mountains facing the desert of Pespire. Small

squadrons were spread out in strategic places to inter-
cept passing merchants and travelers in order to get
food and other supplies that they could not find in the
mountains.

The rebels were alert and constantly at the ready to
defend against the platoons Jonaed continuously sent
to look for them since the rescue of General Melany.
The Mountains of Merendon were intricate and proved
to be a good place for secretive shelter.

"Again?" shouted King Jonaed angrily. "Is there
not a soldier in this entire kingdom capable enough to
capture those rebels?"

"My apologies, Your Majesty," Captain Onan
answered. "We tried, but they know those mountains
far better than we do. It was impossible to apprehend
them."

"How many more apologies do I have to hear,
Captain? Tell me: Do I have to go kill them myself?"
the king shouted angrily.

Captain Onan lowered his head in shame.

"Answer me!"

"I don't have an answer, My Lord."

"Arrange an escort and prepare my horse for
tomorrow at dawn!" yelled the king. "I am going to
have to take care of this matter myself!"

"As you order, My Lord."

"Now get out of my presence!"

"Perhaps there is another way, My Lord King," Eduen interrupted, slinking into the room.

The king looked up to see Eduen. "Wait, Captain Onan," he said.

"What is your suggestion, Eduen?"

"Let me go first, My King. I promise you the head of General Geordano in a sack. I will find them," he claimed emphatically.

"I can't afford to lose you, Eduen. You're my best advisor," the king answered. "They are too many and you are only one. They'll kill you."

"Send me with a small detail of soldiers, My King. I will not fail this time."

Jonaed rubbed his chin for a minute, not saying a word.

"Last time I sent you alone to capture the son of Alexis you almost died," the king said, pointing to Eduen's scar. "I don't want to risk losing my best advisor."

"My Lord, I'll return within a week. Don't worry about me. I know how to take care of myself."

"I am not so convinced."

Eduen waited patiently for the answer to his request.

"So be it," the king said with finality.

The corners of Eduen's mouth curled into a cruel, evil smile.

"You have a week. Leave tomorrow morning... and don't come back to me without the head of General Geordano!"

"As you wish, My Lord."

"Now leave me alone!" the king growled.

Captain Onan and Eduen bowed themselves out of the room.

In his tower, Eduen traced the crevice of the scar Mickail left on his face at their last meeting. "I'll get you for this, Prince Eli. I'll make you pay in ways you can't even begin to imagine. If I can't get you, then I'll hit you where it hurts the most... I'll make your people pay for this."

Prophetess Aledeny rushed out of her home, lantern in hand.

General Geordano heard an insistent rapping at his door.

"Eduen comes, My Lord," said Aledeny, entering breathlessly. "He has promised your head to the king."

"Thank you, Aledeny. I will alert my men. Prepare what you need to leave the camp and take your mother with you. I'll soon send instructions to all the people about where they may take cover."

"Fire the torches!" the guard shouted from atop the rock in the Mountains of Merendon.

The guards posted on the other mountain peaks saw the torch on the northernmost mountain and made haste to light their fires.

The signal of alert let the refugees know that the enemy was coming to find them.

"The warning fires have all been lit, General Geordano," said officer Galel. "Now where shall we tell the people to hide?"

"Direct all the women and children into the caves of Colomoncawa. Send emissaries to Generals Troy and Levy to go and protect our people at the caves. Also send emissaries to General Melany to join me before Eduen reaches the mountains. We must hurry!"

"Yes, General. I'll send them immediately."

"And get the soldiers ready, Officer Galel."

"As you order, My Lord."

"There! That's their signal. They've fired the torches, Eduen," Captain Onan said. "They know we're coming."

"Nothing will save them this time," Eduen answered, sneering confidently. "I will find them, Captain, even if they try to hide underground."

"The soldiers are ready, General Geordano," Officer Galel said. "We'll leave when you're ready."

"Good, we'll head down the mountain immediately. They will not reach the mountains until tomorrow evening. We must ride very quickly if we want to meet them before they meet us."

Eduen turned the Mountains of Merendon into a hell, setting the forest ablaze and killing every living thing in his path. His steps were terrible, leaving a trail of death behind him.

For four days the fire burned and the battle between Eduen and the rebels raged. Generals Geordano and Melany and their soldiers fought with the advantage. They maneuvered easily through the mountains, stalking Jonaed's soldiers, but staying hidden from Eduen. On the second day of the fight, General Geordano and his men were forced to run higher into the mountains. Peering out from behind trees and boulders, in crevasses and caves, Generals Melany and Geordano and their men waited for the enemy to draw near.

Brazenly, Eduen walked ahead of his guard.

Whispering instructions, Geordano prepared tactically for the encounter, "Melany, you circle around behind the guard. I'll wait here for the warlock." She and her rebel contingent quickly and quietly crept into position.

Just as Eduen stepped within arm's reach of their hiding place, the rebels sprang into action. "You seek to destroy the people of the Creator Jhaveh!" General Geordano exclaimed raising his sword to Eduen's throat.

But the warlock had anticipated this lunge, baiting the general, and enticing him into a position of obvious vulnerability. "Tomorrow, General, your head will be at the feet of my king!" Eduen responded, holding the tip of his dagger against Geordano's abdomen. "Now! Get ready to fight! Your life has met its end. Eduen cackled in a shrill and evil voice."

They both pushed back from each other.

General Geordano took up a combat position. He dug his feet into the ground, bent his legs and lifted his sword. "Hmm!" Geordano grunted right back at Eduen, "We'll see whose head rolls first!"

"Aaahhh!" Eduen took out his own sword and made a wild and hard swing at the general.

Clank! General Geordano's sword met Eduen's. *Clank! Clank! Clank! Swiff! Swiff!* Their swords crashed together repeatedly. They were both dangerous fighters.

General Geordano took a couple of steps back. Eduen stood erect, twirling his sword and slowly walking in a circle around General Geordano.

"Are you afraid, General?" Eduen asked, tauntingly. "All this time in the mountains seems to have made you a little rusty? Huh?"

General Geordano eyed Eduen closely, watching his every move. He didn't want to waste any more time going back and forth with this fool.

"It appears that Jhaveh is no longer your protector. Would you agree?"

"Don't you dare speak the name of the Lord, you warlock!" General Geordano shouted as he brought down his sword furiously.

"Ha, ha, ha!" Eduen laughed, intercepting General Geordano's sword with his own. "Your head is mine, General! Ha, ha, ha!"

Eduen attacked General Geordano with vehement resolve, moving deftly and forcing him back even more.

General Geordano whirled around, jumping onto a rock.

General Melany watched the two adversaries' fight from the corner of her eye while in combat with Eduen's small escort. Soldiers from both sides fought valiantly and some fell, wounded or dead, as the intensity grew.

General Geordano and Eduen kept going for several minutes, evenly matching their strength and skills, until Eduen made a very forceful swing with his weapon, breaking the General's sword in two.

General Geordano did not give away his surprise; he stepped away without hesitating or faltering and moved to grab another sword from one of the fallen soldiers.

Eduen did not let up in his cruel pursuit of a fatal opportunity.

General Geordano blindly groped for a sword and quickly bent to reach for one, but before he had time to stand up, Eduen raised his sword in both hands above Geordano's head, poised to attack. Still bent low to the ground, Geordano barely had time to roll and avert the oncoming strike before his face would have been cut in two.

"The general is in trouble!" General Melany said.

Eduen jabbed his sword ever closer to Geordano's neck trying to outmaneuver and overpower him. The two dodged this way and that, each attempting to get the upper hand in the fight.

"Aaaarrr!" General Geordano grunted, doing his best to push Eduen away, because suddenly Eduen was on top and had the advantage.

General Melany thrust her sword into the belly of a soldier and pulled it out quickly. She knew the timing was critical; she had to help Geordano immediately. Sticking her sword into her belt, Melany pulled out her bow, extracted an arrow from her quiver, and fired three arrows in rapid succession.

Zing!
Zing!
Zing!

"Gotcha!" she whispered to herself.

General Melany's first arrow nailed Eduen in his left shoulder. Screaming in pain, he pulled at the arrow and flipped around to face her, just as Melany's other two arrows took flight from her skillfully aimed bow. Eduen caught one of them, but the last of the three pierced his chest. He fell to the ground.

Melany bolted towards General Geordano. Seeing Eduen attempt to stand, she quickly aimed and released two more arrows, one into the chest and the other into Eduen's right shoulder. With those wounds, Eduen dropped again to the ground. Still running towards them, Melany put the bow on her back and reached for her sword in one smooth movement.

"Aaaaahhhh!" General Melany shouted and jumped up, her sword held high above her head.

As Eduen foresaw his death, he tried his best to muster the strength to slither away on his back. A sword pierced the ground between his legs. Looking up, he saw General Melany standing above him, breathing heavily. Her eyes looked into his with ruthless resolve, and he knew in that instant she would not hesitate to kill him.

Eduen scrambled backwards desperately. Blood ran from his chest wounds and his breathing was labored. Unable to get to his feet, he slithered away while steadily holding Melany's gaze.

Suddenly, without warning, he transformed into a dragon! Shrieking loudly, Eduen flew away, wounded and unsteady.

All of Jonaed's men who survived the battle quickly ran away when they saw Eduen take flight.

"Are you okay, My Lord?" General Melany asked of Geordano.

"Yes, I am, General. Thank you. That was very close. I owe you my life now, General Melany." General Geordano gave her a small bow of appreciation.

"I am sure you would do the same for me, General. We are both children of the same land and servants of the same Master."

General Geordano didn't answer. He only raised his sight in the direction of the receding enemies and said, "They are becoming more and more dangerous every day."

Chapter XX

Prince Eli, Liam, and Rolsta flew until dusk on the first day of their journey, landing near a desert in a place called Midian. Walking around for a while, they decided to camp at the foothills of a mountain called the Sinai.

Lighting the fire, Liam and Prince Eli talked about Master Joed, Genesis and all the things they would miss about the Forest of the Musicians. Meanwhile, Rolsta went into the mountains to hunt.

"You ready to get some sleep, brother?" asked Liam.

"Yeah. Hey how long has Rolsta been gone?"

"A couple of hours?" Liam responded.

"Hmmm, let's wait until Rolsta comes back, and then we'll hit the hay," the prince suggested with a degree of worry in his voice.

The brothers waited, but still no Rolsta.

"I'll call him, and he'll come back," Eli said. "Rolsta! Rolsta!" They waited. No answer.

He called Rolsta at least a dozen more times, but Rolsta didn't come.

"Brother, let's go look for Rolsta," Eli said, grabbing a long stick from the fire for light. They searched for his lion for a while but didn't find him. There was no sign of him anywhere.

"It's like he disappeared," Eli said.

"Don't worry, brother. We'll keep searching for him tomorrow. Maybe there wasn't anything to eat in this desert," said Liam.

They made their way back to camp and eventually fell into a restless sleep.

The next day before sunrise, Prince Eli awoke, startled. He didn't sleep well all night thinking about Rolsta and what could have kept him from returning.

"Liam!" the prince said, shaking his brother gently. "Wake up! Rolsta still isn't here."

The brothers packed their things and hiked almost all the way to the mountain to try and find Rolsta, but there was no sign of him.

"What are we going to do now?" asked Liam, ready to give up. Liam rested against a tree. He was tired from so much walking. "Without Rolsta we won't get to the land of the pharaohs. We don't know how to get there. We're lost in the middle of nowhere."

The prince sat on a rock. "Rolsta will show up. I'm sure of it. Let's just rest a little bit and then we will go to the top of the mountain. I'm sure we will find him there."

And they did go to the top of the mountain but saw no Rolsta.

Then the prince remembered the wind. He called to the wind asking him for Rolsta. The wind didn't answer him. Liam tried talking to the wind, but Liam didn't get an answer either.

They kept searching for Rolsta throughout the day until evening came, but it was all in vain. Rolsta was gone.

"I guess we're sleeping here tonight," Liam said.

The sky covered itself with a cloak of black—no moon, just the stars. Both young men felt the desolation of the desert creeping up on them and became desperate for some sign of life.

In the distance something caught Liam's attention.

"Look! Eli!" he said, pointing. "Is that a campfire?"

Eli sat up and squinted in the direction of Liam's pointing hand. "That's what it looks like," he answered.

"There must be somebody over there," said Liam.

"You're right," said the prince, "but it would be worthless to try and get there. We're very tired and besides we won't make it, not even if we walk all night long."

"You're right," said Liam pulling his blanket up underneath his chin.

"We'll go over there tomorrow. Rest tight; we need to recover our strength since walking is our new way of travel. Good night, brother."

Early in the morning they departed in the direction where they had seen the campfire, walking all day under the hot sun until late at night. When they couldn't stand on foot any longer, they fell down exhausted and slept right where they fell.

The next day was no different. The heat rising from the desert sand woke them, and shortly after the two young men discovered they were completely out of water.

It was essential that they keep moving, and so they persisted, putting one foot in front of the other, in search of the place where they had seen the campfire. Just before nightfall, they arrived at the very spot where the campfire blazed two nights before and found nothing but cold, black coals. Nor did they see any sign that someone lived in the area.

There, next to the abandoned campfire's remains, they passed that night and the next day and the day after without mustering the strength to get up and make any forward progress. Eli and Liam thought they would die there next to the ashes, because Rolsta, their only hope of help, wasn't answering them. Neither could they find any water to refresh their bodies. They passed another night feeling hopeless and waiting for their end.

The Spirit of Jhaveh was there.

Chapter XXI

On their fourth day in the desert, Liam and Eli were barely clinging to life. The sand had already covered their unconscious bodies. Fortunately, a caravan of hunters happened to pass by that very spot.

Eli heard voices around him and felt somebody grabbing him by the arms and ankles. His eyes fluttered open long enough to see a group of men milling about and mumbling. They looked worried as they peered closely at Liam and the prince. Eli thought they had a good reason to be concerned but couldn't quite remember why. He closed his eyes again.

Liam also awoke for a few seconds as his body was lifted onto a horse, but he promptly lost consciousness again and acknowledged nothing more.

Two days later Liam woke to the feeling of two soft hands touching his face. Opening his eyes for a moment, he saw a pair of beautiful eyes the color of amber watching him with care and tenderness. The owner of the eyes was washing his face with cool water, but Liam's body was still too weak to react to anything, beautiful or not. He fell asleep again.

The next day Liam woke again and saw two men talking close to him.

Josué, the patriarch of the tribe, and José, his oldest son, discussed their next trip into the city of the pharaohs. Once a year José and his brothers made a trip to the city to sell skins they had collected from hunting and from the slaughter of their cattle and sheep.

Josué was a very dark-skinned man of medium stature, and covering his strong square jaw was a thick beard. Girded above his waist and hanging heavily under his chest, was one of the most prominent symbols of lavish wealth, and he bore it proudly. He also had an excellent sense of humor.

"Uuuuhhhh," Liam moaned.

Josué turned and saw Liam stirring awake. He approached Liam, clapping, speaking in a loud, hearty voice, and laughing boisterously.

"Ah! You wake up at last, son of mine!" he exclaimed joyfully.

"Where's my brother?" Liam asked, dazed.

"Your brother is okay, boy. He's outside talking to the children." Josué extended his hand to help Liam get up from his bed. "But come with me. Everyone's been waiting to meet you."

Even though Liam was still very weak, he made the effort to stand. "I'm really thirsty," he said.

"Of course. Hold on, I'll get you some water." Josué handed him a drinking cup and they both walked out of the tent.

Liam saw his brother sitting on a rock, which he typically did no matter where he seemed to be. Eli was surrounded by children, who were talking and playing with him. But when Eli turned and saw Liam, he immediately rose to his feet and embraced him. "Brother! You made it!"

"Of course, Eli. If I die, what would you do?"

Josué observed them briefly and then left to give them privacy.

"What happened?" asked Liam.

"From what I hear, we lost consciousness in the desert," said Eli. "The sons of Josué were hunting nearby and luckily they found us, very close to death. They brought us here, to their house. The fire we saw was the place where their hunting party had camped that night.

"How long have we been here?" asked Liam.

"Three days," answered the prince. "I woke up yesterday, but you were still too weak to be awakened..."

Liam stopped listening to his brother. His eyes flew wide open as he looked over Eli's shoulder. The prince, noticing his brother wasn't listening, turned around. There walking behind Eli was Samaria, the beautiful youngest daughter of Josué.

"The girl with the amber eyes—she was cleaning my face!" said Liam. He was completely mesmerized, and his mouth hung open. Liam didn't even realize he was spilling the cup of water Josué had given him onto the ground.

"Hello! Hello!" said the prince, mocking Liam and smiling. He moved his arms left and right, snapping his fingers to get his brother's attention. "Wake up! Wake up!" Eli said.

Liam reacted and attempted to utter something intelligible, but he couldn't. His words just came out slurred and sloppy.

Prince Eli burst out laughing at his brother. He understood perfectly what was happening to Liam, because the same thing happened to him on Captain Kaden's ship.

"Wh-who issss sshhheee?" Liam stuttered, blinking his eyes rapidly.

"Hahahaha!" Eli laughed again.

"Eli! Who is she?!" asked Liam again, more desperately this time.

"That's Samaria." Eli still wore a smile on his face. "She's the youngest daughter of the patriarch. She's the one that's been taking care of you all the days you have been unconscious."

"Are you sure I'm not in my bed, still dreaming?"

"The desert is not for you, brother," Eli said, remembering what Liam told him about the sea.

Liam scowled at his brother.

"Well," said Liam, raising one of his eyebrows playfully, "at least we can see her."

They both laughed together.

"Rolsta? What happened to him?" asked Liam, suddenly recalling the events in the desert. He kept Samaria in sight as he talked, watching her out of the corner of his eye.

"He never returned," answered Prince Eli. "I've been trying to talk to the wind, asking him for Rolsta, but the wind doesn't hear me. I don't hear the wind's words either."

"C'mon, children, let's eat!" shouted Josué, interrupting their conversation.

They both went inside the tent and sat at the table with the nine sons of Josué. Estela, the wife of Josué, was cooking while Samaria and her two sisters served the boys.

Estela had prepared something amazing and everyone praised her for it—except for Liam, who wouldn't have noticed anyway. He couldn't take his eyes off Samaria. He smiled at her every time she turned and looked at him, innocently flirting.

"Boys, tell us more about you. Where do you come from?" Josué asked.

"I am Liam, Son of Jore," he answered. "I come from the White Mountains of the South. I belong to the tribe of the Yepoc Indians."

"And I am Eli, the son of Alexis," volunteered the prince. "I am from the city of La Ataviada in the Empire of the Seven King—"

"From La Ataviada?" asked Josué, cutting off Eli's sentence.

"Yes!" said Eli, surprised by the question. "Do you know this place?"

"No, I don't," Josué answered, "but when I was a young boy, my grandfather used to tell me stories about a man that came to our land when he was running away from the soldiers of Pharaoh."

Prince Eli and Liam stopped eating and listened to Josué tell the story.

"His name was Moses," continued Josué, "and he was from the people of the Empire of the Seven Kingdoms. At that time the people of that empire lived under slavery in the city of the pharaohs. By order of the pharaoh, all males born to the slaves were to be thrown into the Nile. Moses' mother, in order to save his life, made a basket and put him into the Nile River.

That basket floated all the way to the aquatic gardens of the pharaoh's house. Servants of the pharaoh's daughter found Moses, and the pharaoh's daughter adopted him as a son."

"After Moses had grown into a young man, he saw an Egyptian mistreating one of his people. Angry, Moses killed the Egyptian. He was forced to run away or be killed by Pharaoh. After a few days on the run, he came here to the desert of Midian, almost dead when he arrived. My family cared for Moses, and after he recovered he began working for my family. Eventually, he married a woman from my family called Sephora, and he became a shepherd."

"Many years later, while watching the sheep, Moses had an encounter with Jhaveh. Jhaveh ordered him to go back to the city of the pharaohs to liberate his people. He went back, bringing with him death and destruction to the people of Pharaoh's kingdom through ten plagues sent by Jhaveh. The pharaoh lost his first-born to one of the plagues, all because he would not release Moses' enslaved brethren."

Liam and the prince looked at each other as Josué told the story.

"If you two ever go to the city of the pharaohs, don't talk to anyone. Don't let anyone see your face," Josué continued, changing his tone and staring directly at Eli, "because they will find out who you are and they will kill you. Your race is hated in the land of the pharaohs."

After Josué finished his story, Liam and the prince remained silent, not telling him that going to the city of the pharaohs was precisely their plan.

What the two brothers didn't know was that the Universe had a different plan for them. They would not get out of the desert so quickly as they thought.

Josué was a very wealthy man. He had herds and herds of cattle and sheep. His family was also great in number. 326 of his sons, daughters, sons-in-law, daughters-in-law, grandchildren, and servants all lived together.

José, the oldest son, and his eight brothers were in charge of managing all the work, giving their servants duties each day. The brothers were also in charge of commerce, taking skins of animals to sell to the cities of the pharaohs.

Outside under the lights of the desert sky, Prince Eli and Liam stayed up late into the night talking with Josué, until he finally said, "Well, boys, I think it's time for me to get some sleep. I'll see you in the morning." Josué stood up and went to his tent.

The brothers sat together quietly for a while. Finally, Liam broke the silence. "So, brother, when do we leave?"

"I don't know how to answer you, Liam. I know we need to recover our strength, but aside from that, I don't know what's next. Rolsta is gone. The wind doesn't speak to us, and I feel a total absence of Mickail."

"What do we do then?"

Eli rested his chin in the palm of his hand. "Until now our trip has been guided by Jhaveh. I guess we wait until the Universe gives us the next step to follow. We don't know how to get to La Ataviada... We don't really have a choice other than to wait for the will of Jhaveh."

Chapter XXII

The days spent with Josué and his family turned into weeks, and weeks turned into months. Eli and Liam fell in love with Josue's family and enjoyed taking part in daily rituals, household chores, and family celebrations. They were in no hurry to leave.

"I have a task for you, Eli," Josué said.

"A task?" The prince raised his eyebrows. "What is it?"

"One of my shepherds is very old and would like to spend the time he has left resting. Liam told me that tending sheep was your duty back in Paradise. I need a shepherd, so what do you say?"

"I don't know how long I'll be here."

"That is of no concern to me. You can be my shepherd till you have to go."

"Okay. I'll do it." Eli was pleased to accept this new responsibility, a contribution he could make in return for the many favors this generous family had extended to him.

As Eli went about his new duties, Liam joined a group of hunters that traveled the land of pharaohs doing commerce for the family.

One day while the prince was in the desert taking care of Josué's sheep, a lion circled in to attack the herd. The prince saw the beast just in time and threw a rock to divert the lion's attention. Snapping his head up in surprise, the lion looked in the prince's direction and started running toward him instead. Eli held his knife at the ready, waiting for the lion to attack. The prince knew that he had only one chance to defeat the savage killer.

The lion approached Eli rapidly, jumped up on his hind legs, and roared. The big cat opened up his front paws, ready to tear Eli to pieces with his sharp claws. Avoiding the charge, Prince Eli leapt to the right and rolled away on the ground.

The lion turned around and charged again. The prince barely had time to get up from the ground. He held his knife ready again and kneeled in front of the beast, looking straight into his eyes as the lion approached. The lion calculated his next move and accelerated furiously, fueled by a desire for blood. Eli waited with knife in hand. The lion leaped again and opened his paws to embrace his prey in a death hug, but the kneeling prince leaned backwards, his back almost touching his legs. The animal flew over Eli, confused at having lost his prey.

As the beast soared just above him, the prince stuck his knife into the lion's chest. Deeply wounded, the lion roared in pain, but the strong and proud animal didn't let the wound stop his deadly intentions.

Immediately, the lion charged again at Eli. The prince didn't have enough time to avoid the attack this time; he was suddenly locked in combat with the wounded and enraged animal.

The lion stood on his back paws, embracing Eli and trying his best to tear Eli's flesh. The prince dodged the lion's open jaws as well as he could to avoid being mauled. Grabbing the lion by his mane and holding his knife in the other hand, Eli plunged the blade into the lion's chest. Over and over Eli screamed with fear and rage as he stabbed at the lion. Losing control of his actions, the prince tapped his own animal instinct for survival and fought for his life with every ounce of strength.

Eventually the lion's wounds took their toll, and the animal flopped limply on top of Prince Eli as the two landed in a heap on the ground. Eli quickly struggled out from under the lion, and when he confirmed that the beast was dead, he gave a shout of victory that carried across the hills.

Other shepherds heard Eli's shout and came running to learn what had happened. When they saw the animal dead on the ground and the prince's torn clothing, they realized what had taken place. From that day on the prince was admired by all the shepherds, who repeated to each other, "Eli killed a lion with only his knife and his staff."

That was not the last time the prince had to defend his sheep. He also came up against a bear and a pack of coyotes, each time with a triumphant outcome.

Liam also stood out in his own way. He earned the respect and admiration of the hunters, Josué, and his children. Samaria especially admired Liam, and he had fallen madly in love with her.

After two years of living in the desert of Midian, the prince had picked up many new skills. He could measure the time of day by looking at the position of the sun in the sky. He knew the schedule of his flock perfectly. He could perceive when a storm was on its way simply by knowing the direction of the wind.

Eli noticed that the birds, the trees, and the light of the sun would behave in a peculiar way, as if they all communicated with each other, and with him, about coming changes in the desert environment. For instance, the wind would warn when there was a sandstorm by lifting small amounts of sand. Eli could recognize easily all these various signs.

During the long quiet times that the prince watched over the sheep, he grew to understand the changes in nature. When the rainy season came, the sheep seemed more energetic — almost joyful — knowing that with the rain an abundance of food and water would come.

The prince could also see how nature patiently repeated its cycle every year. The rain came, making everything grow in fullness; then the time of drought would come, and all the signs of life slowly shriveled away. And just when it seemed that all was lost and the water might never arrive in time to bring life, drop by drop, the rains came and the earth renewed itself with all the vibrant colors of life.

The dry season was a difficult time for Eli. He had to travel deep into the mountains to find green grass for the sheep. There he remained without companionship for long, lonely periods of time with only his memories and desires to keep him company.

Leaning against a rock, Eli felt the soft breeze brushing his face. He could see the wind dancing with the meadows of the mountains, creating waves in the long grass, almost as if he were upon the sea. Steeping himself in the moment, he went back to the ocean in his mind, watching the waves sway in the wind. He could picture the beautiful Princess Kodylynn, with her soft, mesmerizing green eyes and her golden hair beckoning in the breeze.

"Hmmmmmm." Startled by his own voice, the prince opened his eyes, saw the sheep in the meadow, and remembered where he was.

Out here in the desert everything in Eli's life seemed to be nothing more than a dream. The arid, waterless climate seemed to swallow all living things, taking with it the last breath of hope of saving his people. Mickail, the wind, and Rolsta remained silent and inaccessible, their absence unexplained.

Time, how slow everything moved.

Underneath the shade of a cypress, the prince rested on a rock and stared blankly at a dry, empty riverbed. Its bank ended abruptly against the squared-off, vertical wall of a flat plateau.

Eli noticed a ray of sunlight that beamed onto the wall and spread over the entire plateau, forming small fragments of light that separated.

"Looks like the scripture written on the parchment," Eli said aloud.

Suddenly alert, he pulled himself up with his staff and ran toward the wall to find out what caused the lights to form into fragments that way.

"It is the Secret Scripture!" ... *the scripture you will learn in the world of men, little by little.*

When he remembered the words of Master Joed, Eli wanted to run back to his tent without delay and bring back the parchment. He started to gather his things, but then he remembered his sheep and stopped himself. *I can't leave them alone in the desert.*

He was so full of emotion and excitement but calmed down and went back to his herd. "Be patient," he said to himself. "Next time I'll bring the parchment with me just in case this happens again. I'll be prepared."

Eli passed the days and nights like a nomad roaming the desert with his herd. He wished for the hours to pass quickly, so he could go back to the family dwellings and get the parchment.

The night before going back to the community, he lay next to the fire. Staring up at the night sky, he thought of all the things Master Joed said to him: *There are some things you must learn by yourself, and one of them is applying the wisdom and the love of the Universe to your heart.*

"I don't get it," he said speaking into the darkness. "What does 'the wisdom and the love' have to do with the Secret Scripture? Are those things different, or are they the same? Anyway, I guess one day the Universe will reveal the answer to me."

Although Prince Eli didn't yet know, that was precisely what Master Joed had been talking about. Traveling the desert was one part of the whole puzzle, but all Eli could see were the pieces. He didn't see how they all fit together.

The desert and his loneliness made Eli stop, think, and wait. He had to be patient, right along with the sheep, for the rainy season, the natural time of life's renewal. Nature wasn't in a hurry; everything would come along at its precise time.

The sheep became his, and Eli protected them jealously. He knew they were defenseless. If he didn't keep the sheep safe, no one else would. They depended on him daily.

At the same time, his sheep were useful. He needed them just as much as they needed him. They could provide him shelter, company, and sometimes food. Eli walked long distances looking for food and water for the sheep, sometimes forcing himself to keep up the search despite many obstacles and discomforts.

Fighting wild animals to protect his flock made Eli's body strong, and his skin became resistant to the weather.

The sun gave life and made the plants grow, but it also took life. Eli was thankful for the sun's benefits and respectful of its dangers.

Gazing into the vast night sky, sprinkled with countless stars, Prince Eli was totally alone and realized just how small he was. He valued every single drop of water and every single bite of food he brought to his mouth.

Everything in existence had a place and purpose in the Universe. Everything in nature came together to impart wisdom—the same wisdom Master Joed said was needed for a king to rule his people, with love for his brothers and the courage to defend them.

Eli felt Jhaveh had abandoned him, but it was only that he had to understand the nature of the Universe. Eli was living and learning in 'the desert of his life.'

At the first signs of dawn, the prince drove his sheep until he saw the tents of Josué on the horizon. He headed for the sheep corral as fast as he could move the herd.

After closing the gate to secure the sheep, Eli ran to his tent to search for the leather bag his father Jore gave him. There he found it in an old trunk. On his next foray into the desert, he would take the parchment with him. The prince had a week to rest, eat Estela's amazing food, and enjoy some much needed company.

The time to relax passed all too quickly, and soon Eli was again roaming the desert with his sheep. Without being aware of it, the prince drew near to the mountains of Sinai. He had been there with his brother and Rolsta only two years before, and the place seemed familiar to him.

"Plenty of good food around, guys," Eli talked to his sheep. "Eat up."

Prince Eli made camp and rested, far from the tents of Josué. He had been walking since sunrise and it was now late morning. He was tired. Reclining under a tree, Eli fell asleep.

When he awoke, Eli counted his sheep, just as he always did. "One's missing," he said aloud to himself. Worried, he set out to find the lost sheep, but first made sure the others were okay. He followed the sheep's footprints as they headed further up the mountain. Eventually, he found the sheep stuck in a bush. Carefully, he pulled back the branches and grabbed the sheep. Holding the ewe in his arms, the prince felt happy for having found her.

Starting his descent, the prince noticed a rock in the mountainside that had a distinct shape. He went closer to inspect and found something very odd: two matching rectangular impressions—shaped like tablets—had been perfectly carved out of the rocky wall. *That's strange*, Eli thought to himself. He studied the missing stone rectangles for a few minutes, but dismissed them without explanation and returned to his herd.

Unexpectedly, a bright beam of light appeared in front of him, seemingly riding on a strong gust of wind. It made him take a step back, and he whipped around to protect himself. Now facing the strange tablet-shaped spaces, Eli watched as the light formed the Secret Scripture over the cavities in the rock.

When he saw what was happening, he set the sheep down and pulled the parchment out of his knapsack. The prince wanted to compare the scripture on the tablet with the one in the parchment. As Eli opened the parchment, the scripture magnetically flew off the page, crashing against the scripture in the cavity of the rocks!

Immediately, both scriptures melded together and a portal to another dimension opened around him. In that instant, he saw hundreds of messages written in the wind by the sunlight and the dust of the earth as they shifted before him.

The prince heard songs coming from the rocks. He heard the animals communicating and he understood them.

Frightened, Eli let go of the parchment scroll and it rolled shut. Everything stopped. Silence.

Eli dropped to his knees. He could feel in his heart that this place was sacred, so there he worshipped his Creator Jhaveh.

Eventually, he stood up and stacked three flat, smooth stones as a marker to remind him of this place. Then Eli descended the mountain, his heart and face glowing with excitement over his discovery. He wondered how it would come to pass that he would figure out the Secret Scripture.

It was a sweet, calm night. The prince rested at the foot of the mountain and feasted on bread and cheese. Once his hunger was satisfied, he opened the parchment with renewed curiosity.

A moonbeam peeked over the mountain, shooting down to illuminate the parchment. Eli was mesmerized as he watched the cryptic symbols and letters lift off the page and drift with the currents of the wind.

Again the portal opened and revealed its secret messages. All the sounds he'd heard earlier that afternoon played again, only this time the sounds weren't frightening to Eli, just intriguing and mysterious.

He was filled with wonder and amazement that such a marvelous thing could be revealed to him. Inspiration from the Divine shocked Prince Eli's senses, as if something within him anticipated the rainy season of his soul.

From that moment Eli began to unravel the key to the Secret Scripture. Every day that he spent deciphering this cryptic language he felt his spirit aligning with the messages of the Universe.

He read the movement of the light, saw the messages of the earth, and he understood. Each of the pieces of life that he experienced since leaving the Forest of the Musicians flew together into one unified whole. The desert, the sheep, the lonely hours spent in contemplation — all of it collided into one divine picture.

Many months later, while pastoring his sheep, the prince was sitting on a rock and resting his forehead in the palms of his hands, thinking about returning soon to the tents of Josué. His sheep would be sheared and the sons of Josué would make their yearly trip to the land of the pharaohs.

The prince lifted his head for a second, feeling a shift in the air. Much more sensitive now to the elements, he thought something was 'off.' Eli knew how to read the secret language almost to perfection, but he didn't understand the sudden changes in the atmosphere.

Prince Eli ran to the tree where his leather bag hung, believing that his parchment would help him understand what was happening. Just before he reached it, Mickail appeared to him, sitting in the tree's branches. In surprise and shock, the prince fell to the ground.

"Prince Eli," Mickail said, announcing his presence, "how are you?"

"Mickail." The prince got back on his feet and dusted himself off. "I haven't seen you in such a long time. I called to you many, many times since coming to this place. You never answered me. Why?"

"Those were my orders," said Mickail. "Do you remember, in Paradise I said you would have to grow up and become a man by yourself?"

"Where's Rolsta?" asked the prince, now associating his absence with Mickail's words.

"Rolsta is fine. Don't worry about him."

"Will I ever see him again?"

"In Jhaveh's time you will. He's yours."

The prince reached into his leather bag and pulled out the parchment.

"I see you know how to read the Secret Scripture," said Mickail.

"Yes, I do, but something I don't understand just happened."

"That was my arrival," said Mickail. "The atmosphere changes when I appear."

"Oh," said the prince, returning the parchment to his bag.

"How about the wind?" asked Eli. "Will I be able to talk to the wind again?"

"Everything will come back to you when you are ready, Prince Eli. Truly, I tell you, that day is near."

The prince remained silent and sat down by the tree, observing his sheep. "When will I go back to my people?"

"Sooner than you think, Prince Eli."

"What else do I have to wait for before I can go to them? Many years have passed and my people continue to suffer."

"Be strong and courageous," said Mickail. "You have been given the gift not only to read the secret language, but also to write it. Only from your desire springs the ability to write the scripture. You will not return to the Empire until you have attained all that was intended for you by Jhaveh."

"I don't find a way to write the scripture. How will I learn?"

"Keep the words of Master Joed close to your heart." With that, Mickail vanished.

The prince rested his elbows on his knees and recalled the words of Master Joed: "The writer can write sentences into the nothingness using only the pen and ink of his imagination."

A few days later, Eli herded his sheep into an opening on the mountainside to escape from a strong sandstorm. He saw the sand swirling around in the air, and said aloud, "Why not try writing a message with the sand?" Eli focused his mind, attempting to form symbols from the Secret Scripture. "Not the message I wanted... Hmmm."

He was excited anyway, having formed something using only his mind. From that day on he practiced the Secret Scripture until he could create words with beams of light using only the power of his imagination.

Chapter XXIII

Back at the tents of Josué, Prince Eli found his brother Liam lost in thought sitting on the ground outside the patriarch's tent. Curious about Liam's behavior, Eli approached him saying, "Are you waiting for something? Why do you look so worried?"

"Oh, it's nothing," said Liam, extending his right hand as he avoided the real answer to Eli's question.

The prince pulled Liam to his feet. "It's been a long time since we shared anything with each other," said the prince with a sorrowful tone of voice. "I really miss your company, Liam."

"Me too, Brother. But you're always out in the desert. And I am busy with my own duties."

"We should go hunting together again one of these days. Could we do that?" asked Eli.

"Sure," said Liam, who seemed more than a little distracted. "That's a great idea... You know, brother... I, uh, I... need to tell you something."

Eli grew worried. Liam was hesitating uncharacter-istically about something.

"Tell me. Has something bad happened to you?" Eli asked.

"No, no, no, no. Nothing bad has happened to me. It's actually quite the opposite."

"Tell me then..."

"Well, my brother... I am in love with Samaria."

"Ha! I knew that already. Actually everybody knows that." Eli laughed. "You almost had me wor-ried. I thought—"

"—I just asked her father for his blessing to marry her," Liam blurted out.

Eli's smile turned into a wide-eyed look of surprise. "Whaaat? Really? Are you serious?"

At that moment, Josué the patriarch came out of the tent with his wife Estela and daughter Samaria.

"Come, everyone!" the patriarch shouted boister-ously with a grand and welcoming gesture of his arms. "Tonight we will have a celebration, and all are invited!

A crowd of people immediately came to the tent and the prince focused on the patriarch, trying to fig-ure out what the party was about.

"My youngest daughter, my little girl, has found love and is getting married this night! Let us rejoice!" the patriarch bellowed cheerfully.

Eli turned to see his brother Liam looking right back at him.

Liam just shrugged his shoulders, "Uuuuh... Surprise? I'm getting married!"

The prince was shocked and quickly shifted into processing the news that his brother was going to get married this very night. *I wasn't expecting that. I knew he was in love, but... marriage already?* Eli wondered to himself.

Liam pulled his shoulders up again, waiting for something a little more promising than a look of surprise from his brother.

Eli gave up trying to wrap his mind around this news and threw his arms up in the air. "Woohoo!!!" He gave a shout of love and joy for his brother, grabbed him by the arms, and gave him a big bear hug. Liam's face smashed against Eli's face as they embraced.

"Can't... breathe..." Liam squeaked out.

"Ooh, sorry." Eli released his brother from the exuberant hug. They both started laughing and dancing in circles. Josué and everyone surrounding them laughed loudly too.

"Congratulations, my brother!" Eli said hugging him again. "What a beautiful thing you are about to do. Samaria is amazing. You two are made for each other."

Gold candles in jeweled candelabras gave the ceremony a lovely glow. Beautiful silk cloths in all colors of the spectrum hung everywhere. The best wine was served. Ten lambs had been slaughtered and cooked over the fire for the wedding feast. Music played softly, layered beneath the laughter and joy that filled the air. Gifts were brought for the newly wedded couple. The whole community came to celebrate their beautiful union.

The prince sat back and watched his brother's radiant face and cheeks, glowing red with joy. He felt such thankfulness in his heart to Jhaveh because Liam had found a beautiful and excellent woman with whom he would spend the rest of his life.

"C'mon, brother!" Liam yanked Eli out of his seat by the arm and pulled him closer to Josue's family, linked arm-in-arm and dancing around the fire.

"Join us!" they all yelled at Eli.

"I'm only doing this for you, brother!" Eli swung his arms and kicked his legs, joining his brother's new family in lively celebration.

Many hours later, the wedding party slowly came to its end. Everyone went to their tents and fell into a contented sleep.

Just as dawn started creeping over the horizon, Prince Eli had a dream. In it, he was standing on a rock in front of a sword of fire that flew in all directions. A voice from Heaven boomed:

"Invoke in this place the name of your Creator for the innocent blood that has been spilled."

After the voice faded, a powerful force that Eli couldn't describe moved his spirit and lifted him up on the wind above the houses of men. His vision extended so he could see the many seas of the world, all groups of people, and all kinds of man-made constructions and kingdoms.

Then Eli heard the voice of Heaven speaking to him again:

"All that your eyes see I have given into your hands to conquer, Son of Mine. Get up! Leave this place. Your time has come."

The prince sat straight up in his bed. *Truly, it's time to leave,* he said to himself.

After dressing and gathering his things, Eli took a piece of paper and wrote a letter to his brother. He walked to his brother's tent and crept in quietly, leaving the letter and the bags of precious stones Jore had given him close to Liam's head. Taking one last look at his brother, Prince Eli left.

Dear Brother of Mine,

Our Father Jhaveh has called me tonight. My time to leave has come. I must go back to my people and fulfill my destiny.

Your place is at the side of your wife. Tell the patriarch and everyone in his family — your family — that I love them deeply. Ask them to forgive me because I left without saying goodbye.

I am divinely compelled and have been ordered in my dreams to leave immediately. The voice that I heard is one that I must obey.

Practice talking to the wind again, Liam. My ability to do so has returned, and I believe yours will return as well. This way we will always be in touch.

Love always,
Your brother, Eli

The prince saddled his horse and began the journey to the city of the pharaohs.

After three days' ride Eli was entering the gates of the city. "At last!" Eli looked around at the big triangles with four equal sides. "Pyramids! The sailors were right," Eli said aloud with amazement.

Next to each triangle were other structures in the form of animals to honor their gods and the rulers of the land.

Prince Eli put a hood over his head to conceal his face, remembering what the Patriarch of Midian told him: His people were hated in this city.

Walking the streets of the city, he could hear the people speaking in a different tongue. Eli thought it best to pass himself off as a mute. Motioning with his hands, he asked where he could find something to eat. An old man directed him to the marketplace where merchants sold all kinds of things, such as perfumes, fabrics, exotic animals, and food.

Eli soon found a place where he could eat. He tied up his horse and, gesturing to communicate, pointed to an appetizing-looking selection.

Just as he was poised to devour a succulent piece of meat that he'd been served, a trumpet sounded, and all the people around him kneeled, lowering their faces to the ground.

A platoon of soldiers dressed in strange clothes and sharply pointed hats appeared, each one lashing out with a whip and cursing as they passed through the crowded market. The soldiers' actions cleared the way for a carriage that was hefted on the shoulders of sixteen extremely well-muscled men. Inside the carriage rode the pharaoh.

Anyone who did not kneel tasted the ruthless pain of the platoon's metal-tipped whips. Enthralled at the sight of this procession, the prince didn't move a muscle, and one of the soldiers headed right in his direction.

"Kneel before your pharaoh!" The soldier unleashed his whip, but before he could snap it, the prince acted instinctively, caught the whip in the air, and yanked it down forcefully, making the soldier fall to the ground. The other soldiers, seeing what happened, ran to attack Prince Eli and forced him to his knees with a hard punch to the stomach.

At that same moment, the carriage of the pharaoh was passing the quarrel. When the pharaoh saw Eli, he waved his hand, ordering his men to stop the carriage. He opened the curtains and stared at the prince for a minute and asked, "Who are you?"

The prince stared back vacantly. He didn't understand what was being asked of him.

One of the soldiers slapped his face. "Are you deaf! Don't you hear that the pharaoh is talking to you?"

The prince lowered his face, trying to hide it. He didn't answer. The soldier slapped him again on the face.

"Talk to Pharaoh!" the soldier yelled again.

Prince Eli tried to react. When he stood up, they grabbed him by his arms and gave him another hard punch in the stomach. He dropped to his knees again, wincing in pain.

The pharaoh signaled with his hand, telling the soldiers to uncover the foreigner's face.

The soldiers removed the hood and Pharaoh saw from his appearance that the prince belonged to the lineage of Moses.

"Take him to prison!" ordered the pharaoh with a look of disgust. He closed the curtains and made another gesture, and the carriage continued on.

Two more soldiers joined in to punch the prince over and over, leaving him half-unconscious. Then they took him away to prison.

Prince Eli was lying on the floor of his prison cell when Mickail appeared, opened the door, and handed Eli his hooded cape and leather bag.

"Put your cape on and leave this place," Mickail said.

"Where should I go?"

"Go as far away from here as you can."

"Okay, but what direction?" Eli asked again, putting the hood over his head, but he didn't get an answer because Mickail was already gone. The prince picked up his leather bag and darted quickly out of the cell.

Proceeding quietly, he looked down the hall ahead of him. The dim light of the torches hanging against the wall revealed that the guards were dead.

Surely it was Mickail, he thought to himself.

Eli went up to one of the slumped-over guards and took his sword. Quickening his pace, he walked as lightly as possible, trying not to be discovered as he escaped his captors. But just as he stepped outside the prison doorway, another guard saw him, sounded the alarm, and then moved to confront the prince.

The prince killed the guard without hesitation. Four more guards appeared, and he killed them too. Just as quickly, more guards appeared.

Eli had no other choice but to run away. Making a few jumps and quick spins, he reached the roof of the prison. A couple of soldiers copied his feat, and after jumping to the roof, ran after the prince.

Eli ran as fast as he could to stay ahead of them. Tiled shingles shattered with every step. Screeching to a halt, he'd reached the edge of the roof. He looked down and mumbled in self-encouragement, "Not too far," then jumped to the ground.

Immediately, sword-wielding assailants surrounded Eli again. He confronted and killed them with lightning-fast reflexes. The prince looked down the street leading to the prison and saw more soldiers. Aiming his steps in the other direction, he looked up at the sky and saw that it was just about sunrise.

Running with as much speed as he could muster, Eli made it to a marketplace where he tried to blend in and find a place to hide. He scuttled behind some blankets hanging on a pair of thin wooden posts in front of a little store.

The soldiers saw him heading toward the market, and there they began to search for Eli. As they walked past him, unaware of his hiding spot, Eli slowly slid along one of the store's walls, coming out behind the soldiers' back without being noticed. The prince ran into a dark alley behind the market and walked straight into the city's port without even looking for it. Eli looked right and left before coming out of his hiding place to get closer to the docks.

Pharaoh's soldiers soon scattered throughout the port searching for him. A merchant ship was docked and preparing to leave, when the prince saw his opportunity. He concealed himself behind a pile of burlap sacks and waited for the ship to leave.

At just the right moment when the ship was a few meters from the dock, Eli shot out of his hiding place, ran at full speed, and jumped into the water, grabbing one of the heavy lines tied to the ship. Slowly and carefully, he climbed up the rope until he was finally aboard the ship. There he crouched behind some barrels on deck.

He could see the soldiers on the dock screaming and waving their hands, trying to stop the ship, but their attempt was useless. The ship was already too far away.

The prince laughed to himself, satisfied that he escaped. Feeling out of danger, Eli gave a deep sigh of relief, lifted his eyes to Heaven, and silently thanked Jhaveh. He set himself up to hide even better from the ship's crew and made his home there for the rest of the day and night.

The next morning, one of the sailors swabbing the deck discovered him and, before the prince could do something about it, several men surrounded him. He had to surrender. The crew tied him up and dragged him to the ship's captain.

A man with a bitter disposition, a thickly knotted and gnarly beard, dark pockmarked skin from excessive exposure to the sun, and a missing left hand looked at Eli from head to toe. His name was Cody, and he was originally from the Land of the Sons of the Sun.

"What do you think you're doing on my ship, you stowaway?" asked Captain Cody with a gruff voice.

The prince didn't answer because he didn't speak the captain's language.

"Cat got your tongue? What are you doing on my ship?" he yelled, grabbing the prince hard by his chin with his one and only hand. He looked over Eli's face while turning it from one side to the other. "Haaaah, you don't understand what I am saying to you?" he said, releasing his strong grip on Eli's face.

"This man belongs to the race of Moses!" the captain shouted. "Take him to the dungeon!"

Captain Cody spun around to walk to his quarters but stopped mid-stride and added, "Wait a minute. Don't take him to the dungeon yet." The captain came back to inspect Prince Eli's face again. "Your face... It looks familiar... I have seen you before." He paused as he tried to bring Eli's face clearly into his memory. "Aahhhh I know where!" he said aloud. "La Ataviada, at the port. King Jonaed is offering a rather generous reward for your head. Are you Prince Eli, Son of King Alexis?"

The prince recognized the words Alexis and Eli, and replied, "Uhumm."

"Ha, ha, ha, I'll be damned!" the captain laughed as he swore. "Now you can take him to the dungeon," he said and triumphantly returned to his quarters.

The dungeons below the deck were loathsome, dark, wet, and lonely. Eli sat in a locked cell, waiting, until he drifted off to sleep.

Eli awoke to the motion of the ship rocking out of control. Torrential rain and powerful thunder unleashed their fury upon the ocean. The waves rose above the ship, thrashing it back and forth violently without letting up, until finally the ship broke into a thousand pieces.

Prince Eli was stuck below deck, locked in a cell, in a sinking ship! In desperation, he panicked, yanking frantically at the shackles, but they wouldn't come off;

they pulled him under the water. He held his breath for as long as he could, but his lungs couldn't hold under the pressure of the sea.

Eli saw a bright light and thought, *Oh no! This is it. I'm done.* In that instant, before losing consciousness, he saw two bodies forming in the water that looked like angels.

Reaching under his arms, they sped to the surface, lifting him to fill his lungs with the air the prince craved before he died. After sucking in that precious breath of life, Eli passed out.

A few hours later, he awoke. For a second, Eli thought he was dreaming, because a pair of beautiful emerald-green eyes stared into his.

"The Princess of the Waters? Am I dreaming?" The eyes of his beloved leaned over him. Her presence was so clear and intense Eli thought he had died and gone to Heaven. He closed his eyes again, savoring the dream or the sweet reality of Eternal Rest.

Later, when the sun was high in the sky and scorching him alive, Eli awoke and bolted upright, immediately searching for his beloved Kodylynn. There she was, right in front of him, standing by the mast of her raft, and staring back at him with her green eyes. The prince couldn't believe what he saw and jumped back, scared, pinching himself to make sure he wasn't dreaming.

The princess smiled when she saw his uncertainty.

"Are you real?" asked Eli, attempting to poke her just to make sure his mind wasn't playing tricks.

"Yes, I am —" she answered, smacking away his prodding hand, " — real."

The prince looked out over the water, baffled. Pieces of the ship floated everywhere.

"Where am I?" he asked. "How did I get here?"

"We're sailing north. The ship holding you prisoner was shipwrecked during the storm. You were about to die when the angels..."

Watching her while she talked took Eli's breath away. He couldn't believe she was actually talking to him. After so many times sending messages to her on the wind and by the light of the sun, finally his desire to see her was made real. She was only a little less than a meter away from him. He had only to extend his hand and he could touch her. She was real and more beautiful than anything he had seen in his life.

"Ahem," Kodylynn said, clearing her throat to pull back his attention to what she was saying.

"Huh? What?" Eli asked, waking from his daydream.

"Are you listening to me?" she asked with one eyebrow raised.

"Huh? Yeah. I mean, yes, of course, I was listening to you."

The princess looked at Eli, raising her chin a little to let him know she didn't believe him.

"So, where are we?" he asked, redirecting her attention to avoid getting in any more trouble with her.

"We are very close to La Ataviada," she answered, "your final destination."

Every time she talked, Eli stared at her, frozen with rapt astonishment. He couldn't move. As much as he tried to avoid what was coming out of his mouth next, he simply couldn't.

"How beautiful you are!" he whispered, barely able to breathe.

"I know," she said.

The prince smiled back, uncontrollably. "I sent you messages on the wind," he said.

"A lot of them actually," she answered.

"You got them?" he asked. "Why didn't you answer then?"

"It's not our time," she answered. "You have a very big mission in your life. You cannot deter from your destiny for any reason."

"I love you," he sighed. "I have loved you since I saw you on Captain Kaden's ship. I can't stop thinking about you."

An awkward silence hung between them.

But the silence didn't stop him. "Do you love me?" he asked desperately.

The princess smiled with tenderness. "My Prince, it's not our time yet," she said, pointing to the horizon.

He turned around. Here he was at last; in the distance was La Ataviada.

"We have arrived to your destiny," she continued.

He turned back around to face her again, pleading, "Just please tell me if you love me."

She glanced at him and smiled again. "All I'm going to tell you is that one day you will need me, and I will always be waiting for your messages. For now, I shall leave. Go, Prince Eli. Accomplish your destiny."

The prince said nothing more.

They approached the city at the farthest point from its regal gates. There a high wall protected the castle from the ocean.

Eli dove into the water and surfaced. "One last thing, Princess," he said, reaching for the edge of her raft. "Genesis asked me to tell you she's your fan."

Smiling to herself, the Princess of the Waters watched him swim away.

Chapter XXIV

Mercedes, the mother of Aledeny, came running, gasping for air, to the cabin of General Geordano. She yelled, "My Lord, My Lord, come out of your house, please!"

"What is it, Mercedes?" asked the general with concern, standing in his doorway.

"It's Aledeny, My Lord."

"What's going on with her?"

"She's been, well... you just have to see for yourself. She is asking to speak with you. Please come with me to my house."

"Let's go," he accompanied Mercedes without hesitation.

They ran, side by side, back to her house. As soon as they entered, the two saw Aledeny dancing joyfully, tears streaming down her face.

"Aledeny, I'm here," said the general. "You called for me?

Aledeny saw him and stopped dancing. "Yes! Yes, I did call for you, My Lord!" Great joy overflowed in her heart and spilled out in her smile. Calming herself, Aledeny reached out and grabbed both of his hands. Rooted in confidence, she stared deeply into his eyes, saying, "This is what the Spirit of Jhaveh has to say to you, General Geordano:

'Arise solider! Put all your armies together into one. The Day of Redemption has come. Like a thief that comes in the night, so is the Redeemer waiting at the door. He is the One I have chosen from the lineage of Alexis. Join all your men by the feet of the king. Truly, I tell you that in that place you will find the Chosen One who will lead you to freedom. Rejoice, La Ataviada, Daughter of the Empire, because you are a bride once again and your groom is at the door.'"

General Geordano fell to his knees, crying tears of happiness. He worshipped Jhaveh in that place.

Then he left, running to his cabin. Immediately, he sent three men on horseback to give word to the other generals with specific orders to join his troops at the grave of King Alexis at once.

At last, Prince Eli passed through the doors of La Ataviada. He lifted his hood to cover his face and kept his head lowered. Like a thief who walks unnoticed into a house at night, so he walked into the city and down the street leading directly to his once-beloved palace.

Eli no longer saw La Ataviada through the eyes of a little prince, but instead through the eyes of a man. He had grown and transformed physically — no more soft curves to his face or thinness to his arms. His skin was tanned from shepherding, his arms muscular, and his face was now angular. He had grown in wisdom and patience. And Eli had a warrior's heart, beating with a relentless desire to redeem his people.

So many changes... What have they done to you, my beloved city? He thought to himself.

Strange people walked the streets. Altars built everywhere were dedicated to a god he didn't recognize. He could see its form repeated all over the city: a dragon with three heads.

The prince walked to the street where he remembered the marketplace to be. He needed a weapon.

"Good weight and balance. What about the dagger next to it?" asked Eli.

The merchant handed him the sword to test it.

"Good too. I'll take all of them. What's your price?" While negotiating the weapons' price, a nearby disturbance in the street caught his attention.

"What is that?" Prince Eli asked the merchant.

"That is the beginning of a celebration. King Jonaed will be coming down from the palace to the main plaza to give a speech. Then the real festival begins and won't stop for three days and three nights."

"What's it for?"

"Our god. You're not from here, I take it..."

"No. I'm just passing through. Thank you." He walked off quickly before the merchant could ask any more probing questions.

Prince Eli decided to stay in the city for the next three days. *Better lie low,* he thought. *When King Jonaed gives his speech, I'll kill him.*

On the other side of the Empire just outside the Mountains of Merendon, the 12,000 men arrived at the grave of their king. They arrived in smaller groups with their respective generals.

General Melany arrived first.

"Hail! General" said Melany.

"Welcome back," General Geordano answered. "Any news?"

"None, sir. Except that my men and I are ready for battle."

"Finally, the day to fight for our land has come."

"Thanks to Jhaveh," she responded.

"Fourteen long years..." added General Geordano. "We've been here all this time. Jhaveh has kept us and protected us for this moment."

General Melany remained silent. *Yes we have,* she thought to herself. While the General continued talking, she let her own thoughts trail off into the past, remembering the time all those years ago when she watched little Prince Eli leaving with the Divine Warrior and the winged lion.

Melany thought of the years that she spent in prison believing she would die there. Like a waking nightmare, frame after frame of her people's suffering flashed before her eyes: the whips snapping right through their flesh, the endless hours they worked under the hot sun, some passing out and left to die. And the women—General Melany sighed deeply thinking of how they were used for their captors' pleasure and then discarded like garbage.

Jhaveh would avenge each and every one of her people who died by the hand of Jonaed. She cried over innocent and needless bloodshed and now, after all this time, these horrific events would soon come to an end. Jhaveh was ready with flames of fire burning in his heart. His Chosen Redeemer was coming. Tears of release and of hope streamed down Melany's face.

The General had stopped talking a long time ago. "What is it, General Melany?"

"Oh, sorry. Just thinking about what you said, General."

The hour arrived for King Jonaed to give his celebration speech.

The prince walked toward the main plaza of La Ataviada, ready and determined to kill the king. Passing by a dark side street, Eli heard the sound of a cracking whip followed by a scream of agony.

Back-stepping, he craned his neck and could see at the end of the street some men being marched while bound in chains, blood dripping from the raw skin of their beaten backs.

The painful sight hurt Eli's heart so much. He balled his fist, and took a step toward the bloodied men, but then he calmed down and reminded himself that he needed to be patient and not raise any suspicions.

Eli's plan was to get close enough to the king to take him down with the dagger he'd bought from the merchant. He went over the plan in his mind a thousand times since coming to La Ataviada. It was a very simple plan. He didn't really think past killing Jonaed and didn't know what he'd do after that.

Early that same afternoon, King Jonaed stepped up to the platform accompanied by Eduen, who always seemed to be nearby.

Prince Eli advanced discreetly as he weaved through the crowd. Everyone had their attention fully focused on King Jonaed. Eli took advantage of this, discreetly making his way closer to the platform.

I can't miss taking care of Eduen either, Prince Eli thought, remembering his trek into the mountains to find Cain. He wondered whether Eduen would recognize him.

Then Eli grazed someone a little too roughly as he pushed his way past. The man got irritated and made an abrupt move toward Eli. Quickly, the prince ducked down into the crowd to avoid any eye contact with the warlock up on the platform. Predictably, Eduen turned his head toward the disturbance, but he didn't see Eli, who kept himself more alert from that moment on. He continued slowly to wind his way forward to the platform without detection.

The prince was at last close enough to the king to carry out his deadly plan. He reached inside his cape, took out his dagger and raised it to throw, aiming straight at King Jonaed's head.

The sun stood just at the perfect angle on the horizon to catch a ray of light that ricocheted off the blade, creating a brief flash that caught Eduen's eye.

"Watch out, My Lord!" Eduen yelled while pushing King Jonaed down onto the platform. The dagger's trajectory took it flying in the exact path where the King's head would've been, but instead it stuck in a post.

"Stay down, My Lord! Don't move!" The warlock pulled himself up and off of the king.

The prince yanked off his hood, pulled out his sword, and lifted his hands, ready to fight. The crowd parted at the sight of this brave lone warrior, foolish and daring enough to face King Jonaed's many guards.

"Youuuuu!" Eduen recognized him immediately. "Eli, Son of Alexis!" Eduen yelled, looking at the guards. "Kill him! Kill him!"

"I can't believe he would be so stupid to come back here!" Eduen said under his breath.

Immediately an escort of soldiers surrounded Eli. The prince managed to kill some of them, but many more joined the fight.

Fending off the guards as he backed into the crowd, Eli quickly decided to turn and run. He bolted for the nearest house where he dashed inside, barring the door. The soldiers following close behind the prince surrounded the house and then knocked down the door.

Eli crawled out onto the roof and then jumped from one rooftop to the next, leaping and running as fast as his nimble legs would go. *Horses!* he thought, running toward the corral.

"Close all the gates!" yelled Eduen. "No one leaves!"

Reaching the horses, the prince jumped off the roof, rolling over some piled-up hay, and hit the ground inside the corral. Eli popped up onto his feet. The soldiers moved in, blocking his way out of the enclosure and came rushing to apprehend the prince.

Eli raised his eyes and saw the doors of the city closing. He killed two of the nearest soldiers, dodged the others, and mounted one of the horses, galloping out of the corral and down the street.

Eli looked desperately for an exit from the city walls, pulling the reins of the horse this way and that. Ahead of him he saw another group of soldiers. The horse stopped abruptly and reared up on its two hind legs, whinnying.

All the doors to the city are completely closed. Now what? he thought to himself, gritting his teeth. Eli spurred the horse and rode away from the rapidly approaching guards.

The prince looked at the walls of the city as he galloped along, thinking desperately of a way to escape. He knew that on the other side of the walls was the ocean, and at the highest point of the city's wall was a very high cliff. Jumping off would definitely be a risk.

"But it's a risk I'm going to have to take," he announced, decisively refusing to give himself up to Jonaed's men. "C'mon, fella!" he said, talking to his horse, and galloped straightaway to the cliff side wall.

Eli guessed he had only a few seconds to make this jump. Pulling to an abrupt stop, he stood on his horse's back just long enough to pull himself onto the roof of a house, where he rolled, stood up, and ran toward the wall. Eli chuckled and said to himself, "I hope running over the rooftops doesn't become part of my daily routine."

Soldiers swarmed through every avenue of the city, determined to apprehend the elusive Prince Eli. Some went over the walls to wait for him.

The prince kept going from one rooftop to another until he reached a small round tower that he thought would lead to the highest part of the city wall. Inside the tower, he found a spiral staircase and took the stairs two at a time. He could hear the slew of armed soldiers running to catch him as they followed his route across the rooftops.

At the top of the tower, Prince Eli climbed onto the highest part of the wall, peeked over the edge and felt fear gripping his insides.

"There's no way! I'm going to die if I jump." Pulling out his sword, he added aloud, "Better to fight."

But soldiers in overwhelming numbers were closing in on Eli from every direction. He knew it would be impossible to defeat them all.

The prince took a deep breath. He lifted his eyes to Heaven, and, for a moment, everything around him stopped.

He could feel the adrenaline pumping rapidly through his veins. His heart pounded in his chest. Quieting his mind, Eli heard the wind speaking softly: "Don't forget about Rolsta."

He opened his eyes with surprise, coming back to reality. *The wind! Rolsta!* he thought.

The soldiers were getting closer. Acting quickly, he jumped up to the wall's edge. With the soldiers just about to overtake him, he stumbled a little and turned to put his back to the ocean. Then he raised his right hand and waved goodbye to the soldiers. Leaving them with a half-smile, he let himself fall into the emptiness behind him.

"Rolstaaaaa!"

A light shot out from behind the wall.

When the soldiers came close enough to look over the edge, they saw Prince Eli flying away on the shoulders of an enormous lion. The ocean, the heavens, and the guards witnessed his shout of joy for narrowly missing death.

"You are back, old friend!" exclaimed the prince, feeling both excited and relieved. He caressed Rolsta's mane. "I missed you so much."

Rolsta made a small movement of acknowledgment to Eli, and then, guided by the wind, he navigated to the Holy Place over the White Mountains of the North.

Chapter XXV

The moon appeared in the sky, majestically ruling over the stars. Prince Eli and Rolsta came to the Sacred Mountains and landed on a big rock. Emerging from the mist, a sword of fire blazed as it flew in the wind and hindered them from going any further. The prince was a little unsure at first, but then he remembered the dream he had in the desert.

He dismounted, stepped down from the rock, and fell to his knees with his hands and eyes skyward. Eli exclaimed, "Father, Creator of all things, be blessed in Heaven and on Earth. Incline Your ear to Your servant. I invoke You, by the innocent blood that has been spilled among Your people. Stand up, Lord, and fight for us and give the victory into the hands of this humble servant."

Eli sensed a subtle shift in the environment. Then the sword dropped and plunged into the ground right in front of the prince. A moonbeam softly illuminated the Holy Place, colliding with the wind in a silent explosion that sent waves of deathly ominous mist all the way to La Ataviada.

All King Alexis' people throughout the Empire and in the Mountains of Merendon saw the misty light of the moon and felt the shockwaves from its powerful explosion. Breaking the initial silence of their amazed response, they let out a shout so loud that it reached to the desert of Pespire. They knew in their hearts this was the beginning of their victory.

Prince Eli stood and picked up the sword. Its blade was studded with diamonds. "An engraving on each side of the blade..." he said, studying it carefully. "Looks like some kind of celestial scripture. I've never seen it before."

Balancing the blade on his hand, he saw the handle was made of pure gold and adorned with more diamonds, amethysts, rubies, and all kinds of other precious stones.

This way, whispered the wind.

Taking the sword with him, Eli followed the wind's direction and entered the Holy Place where a semi-circle of twelve elders waited for him. Looking at their faces, he made an act of reverence, stepped to the center, and kneeled.

Bartknap, the elder with the highest spiritual authority stood up and said:

"Great is your glory among men, oh Prince of Princes. Blessed you are from the throne in the Third Heaven with an ageless kingdom. The sword you are holding in your hand is the sword of the Creator. This sword cuts to the joints and the marrow, and even to the soul. The scripture inscribed on the sword says

'King of Kings and Lord of Lords.' The horn you carry in your leather bag is the Horn of the War. When it is sounded, the Divine Armies will arise and fight at your left and your right. You are the Chosen Redeemer of all the men of the Empire. Get up now and fight for your people because the Creator has given victory into your hands."

Guided by the Spirit of Jhaveh, the prince stood and walked out of the Holy Place. He mounted Rolsta and flew like the wind to the Mountains of Merendon.

King Jonaed sent his hawks in all directions with a message to his troops to join him immediately in La Ataviada.

Gathered at the foothills of the Mountains of Merendon were General Geordano and his 12,000 men. They all looked to the sky when they saw a strange shadow obstructing the light of the sun.

"An enormous lion with wings!" one soldier cried.

The lion was flying straight toward them. They were all taken aback and prepared their weapons to attack.

"Wait!" yelled General Melany. "Lower your weapons!"

A moment later Rolsta, with Prince Eli in the saddle, landed in front of the army. The lion flapped his wings majestically.

General Melany was filled with joy. *There he is,* Melany thought to herself, *the little prince that was taken from my arms by Mickail fourteen years ago.* Tears welled in her eyes.

General Geordano caught sight of Prince Eli and fell straight to his left knee. Bowing his head, he exclaimed, "Hail Eli! King of the Empire!"

Following the general's lead, the entire army dropped to their knees before the prince, shouting in unison, "Hail Eli! King of the Empire!"

Prince Eli dismounted from the lion's back. He looked at his army, his people, and tried to contain his tears of emotion.

"Arise!" he shouted and approached Generals Melany and Geordano with extended arms. "My brothers and sisters," Eli said with tears in his eyes and a knot in his throat, "finally, I am reunited with you."

"My Lord has come back!" cried General Melany.

All three embraced tightly, overflowing with gratitude. The prince was happy because he was home with his people, and they were overjoyed to finally receive their beloved Redeemer.

After many years of waiting, the promises of Jhaveh came true. The generals couldn't believe that after so much pain and suffering the hope of freedom was finally shining again on the horizon of their lives.

After that warm welcome, the prince and his four generals went to General Geordano's tent.

"What is the state of our army, General Geordano?" asked the prince.

"12,000 men in total, My Lord. 3,000 on horseback, 2,000 archers, and 7,000 infantrymen."

"Do you know exactly what forces we're up against?"

"Yes, My Lord. The enemy's armies outnumber us by more than nine times, but according to my spies only about 25,000 soldiers are stationed in Jonaed's general quarters, near the outlying edge of La Ataviada. The rest of his troops are spread throughout the cities and villages of the Empire."

The prince remained silent for a moment.

"Very well, General," Prince Eli said at last. "Jhaveh has given this army into my hands. Do not doubt that with these 12,000 men we will defeat the enemy."

General Geordano felt his spirit gain strength hearing the prince talk with such confidence and hope, for he was also a man of faith.

"General Geordano, I have one more question."

"Yes, My Lord."

"What happened to my father? I never learned what was my father's fate."

General Geordano looked at the others, letting them know this was to be a private moment of conversation, and they immediately stepped out of the tent.

He looked at the prince somberly, dropping his disposition slightly to say, "Your father died, My Lord."

The prince bowed his head. "I see." He tried very hard to take the news of his father's death without feeling sad. He knew instinctively that King Alexis was dead, but he couldn't help feeling the emotional impact of this news. Sorrow filled his heart. "How did he die?" Eli asked, his voice quivering.

"In battle, fighting at the side of his soldiers, as courageously as any brave and righteous king could."

"Where is his body?"

"Not far from here, about 100 meters from where we now stand."

"I want you to take me to the burial place, but first give orders for the army to prepare. We will leave without delay."

"Understood, My Lord," General Geordano answered and left the tent, ordering the other three generals to organize and mobilize immediately.

Then Geordano took the prince to his father's grave.

When they arrived at the site of Alexis' remains, Prince Eli fell to his knees and cried. Then in a low tone of voice he said, "I swear to you, Father, in this place I will build a statue in your honor that will be seen from all the desert of Pespire. Everyone who passes through these lands will remember the courageous battle you and your soldiers fought for our beloved Empire. I promise you, My Father, My King." Eli stood up and wiped his face.

"General, we will leave as soon as everything is ready."

The prince and the Army of the Empire were en route to La Ataviada. Once again they were fighting for their freedom. Though their army was considerably smaller in comparison to King Jonaed's, Prince Eli was not at a loss for confidence. He did not stumble or falter at what he could clearly see before him.

Jhaveh held charge over the Divine Army, much bigger than any earthly army. He trusted the promise of Jhaveh without any doubts. Their victory was assured.

The trip to La Ataviada would take a few days. Eli instructed Rolsta to return to Heaven for the time being, and then the prince asked for a horse to ride together with his men.

On the other side of the desert, King Jonaed stood in his castle observing his own vast army making its preparations. He stroked his beard and said with an air of pride and arrogance, "We have nothing to worry about." Still, a nagging feeling churned in the pit of his stomach. Jonaed tried to dismiss this sensation by focusing on sound battle strategy and factual evidence.

First, he decided to call in his entire army, certain that the prince would come back to La Ataviada to try and take back his Empire. Jonaed immediately posted 20,000 men outside the city and 5,000 inside its walls. The rest of his army would arrive as support, shortly after the fighting began.

He knew of no other king or empire that could match the number of his soldiers. The Imperial Army of King Alexis would be exterminated once and for all.

Prince Eli rode on steadily with his men, knowing perfectly well he was heading straight into a trap. His men were worn down from the fourteen years they had passed in the mountains, but they had warriors' hearts and they loved their land profoundly.

Even with all the odds calculated and examined, Eli firmly believed in his heart the promise Jhaveh had made to him. He didn't know how the victory would come; he only knew that it would come.

All the years he prepared and trained, since he was a nine year-old little boy, taught him to trust in the word and promises of Jhaveh. The desert taught him that when he thought everything was over, and that his dreams were nothing more than dreams, Jhaveh would give him victory, even when Eli least expected it.

The days passed as the Imperial Army crossed the desert of Pespire, advancing steadily forward to La Ataviada. The soldiers played drums every now and then, singing songs to the Creator and giving Him thanks for a new opportunity to fight for their freedom.

Chapter XXVI

The long awaited day for the children of the Empire had come. As Prince Eli and his Royal Army approached La Ataviada, the sun set high in a cloudless sky. Only the blue of the sky's splendor covered the firmament.

King Jonaed prepared his men for the imminent attack and stood abreast of them, as was his strategy to manage his troops.

Eduen stayed in his tower, formulating a Plan B, and watched the troops prepare for battle from the window of his parapet. Eduen knew this war would not be like any other Jonaed's forces had fought. They were confronting the Army of the Empire but also the will of Jhaveh to free his people.

Anticipation filled the closing divide between the two armies. The soldiers of the Empire were nervous, because the army in front of them had already defeated them once.

Finally Prince Eli gave the order, and the drums and the trumpets sounded their challenge. When the instruments blared, the Army of the Empire began singing in unison:

"Blessed is the Lord, Jhaveh, who has broken the chains of our captivity, and today he has given into our hands our enemies. We will be free in the name of the Creator."

The drums, the trumpets, and the song of the soldiers came to an abrupt and unified silence, infusing the environment with patriotism. A feeling of certain victory filled their hearts and spread into the air surrounding them. This was their land, their city, and their battle to be won.

The prince raised his sword to Heaven, the bejeweled and sacred sword of Jhaveh. The blade shone brilliantly with a light more resplendent than the sun.

Jonaed's legions quivered with fear when they saw the shining sword held high. It represented far more than a weapon. The sword was Truth and Justice. It was Jhaveh. Its luminous blade struck fear into the heart of every soldier who was an enemy of the Empire.

Because Eduen's heart was above all wicked, the luster of the Divine Sword hit him with such power that he was thrown to the ground several meters from his perch at the window. With no chance to hide from the shockwave of the sword, this blow angered Eduen even more.

The soldiers of the Empire marveled at the prince's dazzling sword and felt a surge of confidence, no matter their numbers. Their fear of Jonaed's forces evaporated before the glory of Jhaveh's luminescent blade in the hands of their valiant leader.

Prince Eli addressed his soldiers, shouting, "Brothers and sisters of mine, children and priests of the Empire of the Seven Kingdoms! This day our Creator has defeated the oppressor. Rise in courage and fight for your freedom until death. Be fearless because Heaven has given us the victory without yet raising our swords!"

Riding to the front of his army, Eli spurred his horse and shouted, "For the sons and daughters of the Empire!"

Eli rode straight ahead at a full gallop, his heart overflowing with courage, ready to encounter the swords and spears of his enemy. The army behind him gave a battle cry that could be heard within the city walls. Slaves and prisoners yelled back from inside with their own cry of war, and their spirits swelled with hope and joy.

Enemy soldiers inside the gates, hearing the shout, felt their opposition was somehow greater in number than they had been told.

King Jonaed's army charged forward to confront the soldiers of the Empire. As each of the opposing forces moved dangerously close to the other, the fight could no longer be avoided.

Prince Eli spurred his horse to jump, soaring over the enemy's front lines and missing the spears that were inches away from piercing his flesh. He swung his sword wildly, making pieces of any resistance in front of him.

Spears and arrows protruded from the bodies of Jonaed's soldiers. They screamed in pain and anguish seeing severed arms and heads of their comrades lying on the ground. The intensity of their groans increased as the wounded and dying grew in number.

The generals of the Imperial Army made headway through the mass of Jonaed's men. General Melany fought fearlessly, putting her heart into every strike of her sword. No one that opposed Melany the Valiant remained alive.

With every clink of metal crashing against metal, with every thrust and turn of a sword, the stain of blood grew on the battlefield. In a strange phenomenon that none of Jonaed's men could comprehend, they fell easily and in great numbers while their opponents thrived.

Suddenly a spear flew through the air, felling Prince Eli's horse, but Eli jumped off and landed on his feet. Without flinching, he continued fighting as if nothing had happened. Nearby, General Geordano followed his king's lead, leaving his own horse, and fought on the ground alongside the prince.

Standing at the center of his army, King Jonaed could see that everything was not going the way he hoped. "We're being annihilated!" Irate, King Jonaed unleashed his wrath on anyone standing near him. "Can you tell me how we could possibly be overwhelmed by Prince Eli's small and aged army? Huh? I want answers now!" he barked. No one knew what to say, and everyone scrambled to another location to dodge the outpouring of Jonaed's anger.

Hours passed and the battle raged on. Jonaed's men were dying by the droves, yet not one of the Imperial Army's soldiers had been harmed. It was as if a supernatural force protected them, and with every passing minute, they pushed back Jonaed's crumbling kingdom.

As he looked at the carnage surrounding him, Prince Eli knew the forces of the Empire were winning the battle. And then he heard a trumpet sounding from far away.

King Jonaed gave a deep sigh of relief. *Victory,* he thought to himself. *My reinforcements have arrived just in time.* Over 80,000 men came from all directions to join the battle. They screamed in fury and rage, thirsty for blood.

The Army of the Empire stood surrounded again, a replay of two perfect ages before. The soldiers were stunned.

For a moment Prince Eli doubted, unsure of what would happen next. Into his mind flashed the words of his beloved Princess of the Waters, "One day you will need me and I will always be waiting for your messages."

Determined, he stuck his sword in the ground, kicking up dirt. Making the symbols of the Secret Scripture, he whispered into the wind a message for Princess Kodylynn. "Take it!"

The message vanished and the prince turned back to face the battle with a surge of energy.

The Imperial soldiers felt the massive army closing in around them, but taking a cue from their prince, they fought with steadfast vigor.

A deafening clap of thunder erupted from the ocean, and everyone from both armies froze in their fighting stance. A colossal wave lifted out of the water, and every warrior watched with wonder as the ocean transformed into a legion of angels. Then, flying over the city and terrifying Jonaed's men, the angels joined the Imperial Army in their fight.

"Every last drop of your blood, Jonaed, to pay for the tears and pain of my people—I will take nothing less!" Prince Eli pushed defiantly through the lines of enemy soldiers, killing all who blocked his path. He was resolute; he would reach King Jonaed.

The war tarried into the night; the moon and the stars witnessed the heavenly massacre.

Prince Eli did not stop for any reason, not even to rest. When the horizon reddened, breaking into a new day, he finally caught sight of Jonaed. The king locked gazes with Eli and jumped from his carriage, bent on eliminating the prince once and for all.

The prince, without dropping his gaze, hurdled over some of the soldiers and pushed everyone else out of his way, his eyes focused on only one man. Eli raised his sword to his ear, with his right foot forward, only inches away from King Jonaed.

"Prince Eli, so nice to see you!"

"I'm not here to talk. Draw your sword!" Prince Eli challenged with fire in his eyes.

"Well, if you insist, then let us begin!"

In one swift movement, King Jonaed pulled out his sword and slammed it against Eli's, creating a shower of sparks. Everyone around them parted as the two leaders began their duel. Both were very skilled swordsmen, and the fight persisted with each man slashing and leaping and twisting and dodging with precision.

Upon the walls of the city, Eduen had been busy concocting a curse to invoke the help of his own god, the Blackfire.

A dark cloud formed over the morning sky, originating from Eduen's place in the tower. High-pitched screeching filled the ears of all the warriors. From every direction, winged creatures infested the sky. These skeletons of hell—made of only bones; claws, and black scales—shrieked and breathed plumes of fire down to earth to announce their presence.

Riding upon the creatures were demonic souls, clothed in shadows of death with green flames of fire for eyes. Leading the way was a three-headed dragon, the Blackfire in beastly form.

These supernatural enemies were the ones Jore spoke of that had once been Divine Warriors, but rebellion against their Creator had transformed them into demons.

As growing hoards of dragons and death shadows joined the fight, Kodylynn's angelic army was vastly outnumbered.

When the prince saw his winged adversaries, he shouted to summon Rolsta. Eli knew instinctively that he must deal with Jonaed immediately. Lifting his sword above his head, he shouted, "Aaaaaahhhh!" A divine power coursed through the prince's veins.

King Jonaed raised his sword, attempting to block the prince's blow. Eli wielded the power through his sword, pulling it as far back as he could before swiftly plunging its blade into the belly of the king.

Letting out a low moan, Jonaed dropped his weapon. He touched his wound and saw his hands covered in blood. Staring into Eli's eyes, the fallen king wanted to say something to him, but it was too late for him to form any words. Jonaed fell to the ground, dead. The prince was confused to see that King Jonaed's eyes showed no anger, fury, or vengeance as he took his final breath. This was not what Eli expected.

The battle crisis loomed all around him. Wasting no more thoughts on Jonaed, Eli mounted Rolsta. The winged demons that filled the sky were now his to fight. The war was no longer a human war but a supernatural one.

"Fly, Rolsta! Fly!" Prince Eli shouted.

Rolsta shot forward and Eli confronted the Blackfire and his army, cutting through the death shadows with his sword. Each time his blade touched them, the shadows vanished, but even more of them quickly populated the sky.

"There are so many!" Prince Eli became overwhelmed with his task.

The golden horn! the wind whispered.

With that message, Prince Eli's eyes lit with new hope.

Bartknap had assured Eli at the Council of the Twelve Elders: "At the sound of the horn the Divine Armies will come, and to your left and your right they will fight."

The prince tore the golden horn from his belt, but just then the three-headed Blackfire rushed Eli, forcing Rolsta to make an abrupt maneuver. The prince almost lost his balance, and the golden horn plummeted to the ground, landing next to General Geordano.

Geordano picked up the golden horn. He looked up to see Prince Eli make a nosedive to grab it, with the Blackfire following close behind him. The general threw the horn into the air. Eli caught it, instantly put it to his mouth, and blew.

The horn gave a resounding blast. When the shadows heard the powerful sound, they covered their ears and trembled with fear. The three-headed dragon thrashed in the air screaming; the beastly Blackfire knew what was coming.

North of the Empire, in the Sacred Mountains, the Divine Army's trumpet sounded its response just a few seconds after the summons of the golden horn. Countless winged lions filled the skies and flew toward the battle. The powerful flapping of their wings could be heard at a great distance. And flying above the lions was an army of angels. The Divine Warriors had arrived.

The angels were of inconceivable height. All had diadems of pure gold on their foreheads, and their swords were also of pure gold.

Their appearance rolled back the dark clouds and gave way to the blinding brilliance of the sun's rays reflected off the clothes of the Divine Warriors. An extraordinary light stretched to Heaven and struck the ground, making the earth rumble with its forceful impact.

Over the battlefield, the winged lions violently confronted the skeletons of hell, sticking sharp claws into their scales. The Divine Warriors and the death shadows were locked in combat, just as they battled at the beginning of all times.

When the enemy soldiers on the ground saw their king was dead, they lost their will to fight and raised their arms in surrender. But the battle in the sky continued. The Divine Warriors and the death shadows shook the earth with the crashing of their weapons.

Prince Eli had an idea. He flew over the ocean, with the Blackfire pursuing him. Snap! One of the dragon's heads barely missed impaling Rolsta on his sharp teeth, but Rolsta sped up, out of the Blackfire's reach.

"I want you to circle back around, Rolsta. Fly over the top of the dragon. Got it?"

While Rolsta navigated directly over the dragon, the prince jumped, landing on the Blackfire's back and grasping his scales to hold on. The dragon tried to shake Prince Eli, but Rolsta attacked him from the front, sinking his claws into the dragon's chest. The Blackfire made a violent move and smacked Rolsta with his tail hard enough to knock him out. Unconscious, the lion fell into the ocean.

Seeing an opportunity to assist, Kodylynn's angels quickly rushed in to bring Rolsta to the surface.

The prince strengthened his grip on the dragon's back and, with difficulty, climbed all the way to the junction of necks where the Blackfire's three heads converged. Pulling out his sword, Eli severed one head. The Blackfire screeched in pain and began to fly aimlessly.

Unseated, Prince Eli slid down the dragon's scales, heading straight for the water. Determined to hang on, the prince hooked his arm around one of the Blackfire's necks. He was looking right at the dragon's chest. Taking advantage of his new position, Eli swung his body and with one clean swipe cut off the Blackfire's second head. Now with only one head remaining, the dragon and Prince Eli tumbled into the ocean and began wrestling furiously in the water.

Mickail flew directly into the fight carrying a great chain of light. Encircling the beast with his chain, he fettered the Blackfire and dragged him to the bottom of the ocean, confining the beast to his abysmal prison.

Meanwhile, Rolsta came to. The lion swam to pull Prince Eli from the water and onto his back. Together they watched Mickail take the beast to the bottom of the ocean.

"Fly Rolsta!" Prince Eli said.

From the corner of his eye Eli spotted a familiar glow on the ocean. His beloved Princess of the Waters gazed at him, standing as always at the edge of her raft. He watched her until she became a tiny speck on the ocean. Eli then turned his attention to his people as he and Rolsta returned to the battlefield.

At the same instant the Blackfire was imprisoned in the water, the death shadows in battle with the Divine Warriors disappeared in the wind. Eduen made his own way of escape. Transformed into the beast he was, the warlock flew away from the tower.

The soldiers of the Empire saw their Redeemer flying overhead on the lion's back and raised a shout of victory and freedom that rang all the way to Heaven. Then Rolsta landed, lifting up a cloud of dust with the flapping of his wings.

Mickail surfaced from the ocean floor and flew to Prince Eli's side and said simply, "It is done, Prince Eli." He then led the Divine Army back to the heavens.

After Mickail and the angels departed, Eli dismounted and looked at Rolsta eye to eye. "So long, my dear friend," he said caressing the lion's mane. "You and I are one and the same. Our friendship will last forever. You may go now."

Rolsta answered by lowering himself onto his front legs and then flew off and disappeared into a beam of light.

Prince Eli stood in front of his army, raised his sword, and shouted, "Jjjhhhaavvveeehh!!!" His soldiers responded with their own powerful cry of victory, all raising their weapons to the heavens. Their hearts were filled with expectation and many other joyous emotions.

Prince Eli addressed Jonaed's surrendering soldiers: "Your king is dead. Your armies could not withstand the power of Jhaveh's desire. At this time, you may expect me, as the rightful victorious king, to enslave you and your families. However, I will not. If it is your desire, I offer you the opportunity to stay in this Empire free and clear of your past transgressions. Your people have my permission to occupy the lands of the Occident."

Captain Onan, King Jonaed's highest-ranking officer, addressed the prince. "You are an honorable man, My Lord. My sword and my loyalty are at your feet, My King." Falling to his knees, Onan shouted, "Hail Eli, King of the Empire!"

Then, one by one, the rest of the defeated soldiers began to kneel until the entire army was on their knees. Onan's comrades responded in thunderous unison, "Hail Eli, King of the Empire!"

"Arise and go in peace," King Eli said, and then he turned to face La Ataviada. "My beloved city, I walk through your gates in long awaited triumph."

Eli entered La Ataviada followed by the victorious soldiers of the Empire.

Chapter XXVII

"By the desire of Jhaveh and the authority given to me, I crown you King of the Empire of the Seven Kingdoms!" Bartknap loudly declared as he lowered the crown onto Eli's head. "Arise, King Eli, beloved Son of the Empire!"

Rising slowly, King Eli turned to see his people. Immediately, a chorus of joyful shouting and applause filled the royal chamber and spread like a tidal wave of praise throughout the entire city of La Ataviada.

"Brothers and sisters!" Eli shouted. "Today, a new epoch begins. Times of prosperity and peace lie ahead. Let us delight in the freedom our Creator has been pleased to give us! Blessed be the Lord forever!"

The shouts of joy intensified.

"Let the celebration begin!" Eli exclaimed.

Each and every citizen of the Empire joined in the festivities to commemorate victory over the forces of Jonaed and the coronation of King Eli. The royal palace was filled with the sounds of joyful music and dancing. Tables overflowed with more than enough bread and wine for a feast; fruits and vegetables were gathered, prepared, and spread in delicious array; and thousands of lambs and cattle were slaughtered to satisfy the hunger of all.

King Eli sat back in his throne with a great smile of joy spread across his face. Finally, after all those years of waiting, his dream of redemption for the Empire was a reality.

While Eli sat quietly basking in the happiness of his people, a floating light — visible only to him — suddenly appeared in front of him. The light grew into wings, then a body, and finally a face. It was Mickail.

Brilliant light flowed around the Divine Warrior. Bending forward slightly toward the king with his left hand over his chest and his right arm extended in a salute, Mickail smiled with complicity. "Well done, King Eli," he said with a wink and a twinkle in his eye.

The king responded by smiling back at Mickail and bowing his head just a little. As the light and image faded, Eli's heart filled with gratitude for the warrior angel, his lifelong protector and his oldest friend.

The celebration lasted throughout the night, and as the hours passed, the king began to think of his family in Paradise: Jore, Patypa, and Liam. He especially missed his beloved brother. How Eli wished that Liam could be there with him on this most important day of his life! A melancholy mood began to fill his heart. "I have to go visit my brother soon," he said to himself.

Deciding that he wanted to be alone, accompanied only by the memories of his parents and his brother, Eli told General Geordano to make sure that he was not disturbed. He rose from his throne and went outside to the balcony.

Peacefully alone with his thoughts, King Eli looked up at the moon. How serene she was in the sky with the light of all her splendor caressing the lands of the Empire, as if sharing the happiness of the beloved people of Jhaveh!

Then Eli watched with wonder as his very first message from Princess Kodylynn slowly began to unfold in a moonbeam.

"Our day is getting closer, My King," read Kodylynn's moonlit inscription.

King Eli read the message, and the smile spread across his face told him his adventures weren't over yet.

Made in the USA
Charleston, SC
05 June 2014